The TURNGLASS

GARETH RUBIN

SIMON &
SCHUSTER

London · New York · Sydney · Toronto · New Delhi

First published in Great Britain by Simon & Schuster UK Ltd, 2023
This paperback edition first published 2024

Copyright © Gareth Rubin, 2023

The right of Gareth Rubin to be identified as author
of this work has been asserted in accordance with the
Copyright, Designs and Patents Act, 1988.

1 3 5 7 9 10 8 6 4 2

Simon & Schuster UK Ltd
1st Floor
222 Gray's Inn Road
London WC1X 8HB

Simon & Schuster: Celebrating 100 Years of Publishing in 2024

Simon & Schuster Australia, Sydney
Simon & Schuster India, New Delhi

www.simonandschuster.co.uk
www.simonandschuster.com.au
www.simonandschuster.co.in

A CIP catalogue record for this book
is available from the British Library

Paperback ISBN: 978-1-3985-1452-2
eBook ISBN: 978-1-3985-1451-5
Audio ISBN: 978-1-3985-2298-5

This book is a work of fiction.
Names, characters, places and incidents are either a product of the author's
imagination or are used fictitiously. Any resemblance to actual people
living or dead, events or locales is entirely coincidental.

Typeset in Sabon by M Rules

Printed and Bound in the UK using 100% Renewable
Electricity at CPI Group (UK) Ltd

MIX
Paper | Supporting
responsible forestry
FSC® C171272

For Hannah

The TURNGLASS

It was the lark, the herald of the morn,
No nightingale: look, love, what envious streaks
Do lace the severing clouds in yonder east:
Night's candles are burnt out, and jocund day
Stands tiptoe on the misty mountain tops.
I must be gone and live, or stay and die.

Romeo, *Romeo and Juliet*, ACT III SCENE V

Chapter 1

Los Angeles, 1939

Ken Kourian's eyes, pale green like thirsty grass, bent to the coffee-stained page in front of him. It smelled strongly of coffee too, as if someone hadn't just spilled his drink on it, but had marinated it in the cup for twelve or fourteen hours.

'It's called *The Siege of Downville*.'

'I see, and I—' began Ken.

'You're a soldier just back from the War.'

'Which one?'

'What?'

'Which war? Great War or—'

'Civil. Civil fucking War.'

'Okay. And am I Confederate or—'

'Yankee! You're up for a Yankee. You think ... look, kid, are you gonna read the lines or am I gonna read them for you?'

This was the best chance he had had in months and there were people lining up outside the room, so he put on a Yankee accent and read the lines. They were something about being injured and needing to see his sweetheart one last time before he died. They seemed badly written to him, but he didn't want to rush to judgement because he had never been in a picture and even his stage credits were only those from college and a couple of years in second-rate shows around Boston.

'Where're you from?' the overweight man behind the desk demanded, staring at him as if he should have a luggage label on his forehead.

'Georgia.'

'Georgia!' He scratched his midriff through straining shirt buttons. 'Then why the hell'd they put you up for a Yankee? Why not one of the slave-keeping sons a'bitches from the South?'

'Beats me,' Ken said. He gazed at the script.

'Beats me too.' The man, the assistant producer, tossed a cigarette butt aside into a bucket of water, where it floated, seeping a brown trail. 'Look, son, it's not your day. Come back another time.'

'I'll be sure to,' Ken replied. And he would. He wasn't one to bow to pessimism, because Ken Kourian was twenty-six and it hadn't yet set in like damp.

As a boy in Georgia, he had seen the distant Blue Ridge mountains and thought of them as separating him from Greek wars and journeys across seas. Then, as he had gotten older, he had come to see them as the hurdle before an unidentified 'more to life'. So he had set out on that journey, as the first in his family to go to college; and now, as a five-year hangover, he was repaying his parents and two banks for the cost, a few bucks at a time.

He picked up his hat, wished the movie well and left through the studio lot, still holding the bad script. Two men with stuck-on moustaches the size of house cats walked past wearing Union uniforms. Ken wasn't sure whether to envy them or pity them for getting into the picture.

Outside the studio, a streetcar was rolling along the road and Ken jumped aboard hoping that it was heading for the beach. Even after months in the city, his understanding of the geography of Los Angeles and Hollywoodland could have been drawn on a playing card. His home town had more elm trees than people and the elms didn't rush around, barging you from the sidewalk, in a hurry to get somewhere to be told to go somewhere else. Sure, he had also been in Boston for eight years – in college and then a little tutoring and a little acting – but his feet still hankered for a path of soft leaves underfoot. In California, wet sand would do as well, however.

'Is this going towards the beach?' he asked the conductor.

'What?'

'The beach.'

'The beach is ten miles in the other direction, pal. You want the beach, get off this car and take one going the other way. Ride it eight stops and then change to another.'

It sounded too complicated. 'Where's this one going?'

'This one? Where do you think it's going? Downtown. Along Sunset. So, you want Downtown or you want the beach?' A woman in a seat was offering a five-dollar bill for a ticket and insisting the conductor take it. 'I can't change that, sister. The fare's only a dime.'

'Well, you should have said that before I got on,' she replied huffily.

'Before you got on? How would I do that? I was in the vehicle, not beside you on the street. Now, do you got change or not?'

'I'll go Downtown,' Ken told him.

'Downtown is ten cents. And I don't got change for a five-spot.'

He paid his money and rode the car.

He had been riding for about ten minutes, watching the passengers get on and off, trying to work out who they were and if they worked in the movies or if they were cobblers or accountants or longshoremen or stockbrokers, when he spotted an endless ridge of trees.

'What's that?' he asked the conductor.

'That? You don't care what that is. You're going Downtown.'

'I'd like to know what it is.'

The conductor groaned. 'That's Elysian Park. Stay away from there.'

'Why?'

'Full'a boogies from Lincoln Heights. Take your bill-fold, won't give it back even if you ask nice.'

'Oh,' he said. His dad had employed coloured labour alongside white workers on the farm, paying the same rate, but Ken had given up trying to evangelize this system to his high-school class, who stared and then laughed when he put the idea in front of them. At college, a few had nodded knowingly at the idea and said that yeah, it was the future, for sure, but then hired negro butlers at two-thirds the going rate for men with pink skin, leaving Ken wishing he had saved his breath. 'I think I want to go there anyhow.'

'Whatever you say, pal.'

And Ken Kourian, point-jawed, six feet and an inch tall, with healthy farm-boy muscles and a degree in literature from Boston University, jumped off the streetcar and strolled towards the line of elm trees.

The park was cool and lush on a day hot enough to melt automobile tyres. The sensation of grass and fern under his feet soothed him like a drugstore balm. Whatever had ailed them, making the soles bristle in his stiff new patent leather shoes, disappeared, and he could have been bare-foot, padding through the undergrowth.

How many trees were there? Ten thousand? A hundred thousand? Ken appreciated the shade, needing to cool down after a frustrating couple of hours. Paramount were casting for a new epic, he had been told at the studio gate. If he put his name down, he might be seen for a small part.

It would be a 'cattle call' casting and that didn't sound good, but it was better than being told to go boil his head.

'Well, I've worked on farms,' he said.

'Then you'll be right at home.'

He hadn't gotten the job. Sure, it was a disappointment, but there would be other chances. They said that the pictures were getting bigger each year. Bigger pictures meant bigger casts. He would stick it out, and in the meantime he had a job writing advertisements for the *Los Angeles Times* and that was enough to pay his modest rent. And his plan was that hanging around the paper's entertainment desk he would hear about the new movies in development, so he could run up to the studio early and ask to be seen. Yeah, maybe it would work.

He walked through the heat of the April afternoon. The birds in the trees were kicking up a hullabaloo before taking off in huge flights in search of food or water or whatever else a bird wants on a hot day in California. He wondered what his own plan for the afternoon was. Keep walking until he stumbled into the town proper or hop back on the streetcar to his boarding house beside a grocery store that he suspected of selling home-distilled hooch from the back door? He had toyed with the idea of calling in there himself some time and seeing what was on the menu.

He just kept walking.

By the time he looked up again, he had walked right through the park to the other side and road noises were rubbing around him like mosquitoes. He thought about turning around and losing himself among the trees again, but he was thirsty and beside the road a diner's neon lights were inviting him.

Ken strolled in to find himself bang in the middle of the late luncheon rush, and the popularity of the place meant there was only a single table left. It was in a corner booth where the fake leather that probably came from a factory a thousand miles from the nearest cow was a deep gold colour. He went over, but as he came close he saw a girl already there. She had been sitting against the wall, out of sight. She looked like she had been trying to keep a low profile.

Ken paused. But she turned two heavy brown eyes up at him expectantly.

'Can I sit here?' he asked.

'Sure.' She said it slowly, like she might change her mind halfway through.

He nodded in thanks and took the seat. She was sipping white coffee and flicking through a magazine about talkies. She was slim, with a pert mouth that looked like it was recoiling from a too-hot drink, and wore a cream turban, a cream blouse and tight cream pants. Ken reached across for the menu in a glass pot at the edge of the table.

'The peach pie is a specialty,' she told him, without waiting for him to ask.

'Does that mean it's good?'

'It just means it's a specialty.'

A waitress appeared at his elbow with her notepad ready. 'I'll have the peach pie,' he told her. 'I hear it's a specialty.'

'Sure it is,' she muttered, writing. 'Anything else?'

'No.'

She pointed at the girl opposite with her stub pencil. 'You covering her check?'

The girl in cream met his gaze. Something in hers said that if he didn't cover it, no one would.

'Okay,' he said.

'I hope it's worth it,' the waitress said, walking away.

Ken and the girl stared at each other for a few seconds. 'Thanks,' she said.

'Don't mention it.'

'But I have to, don't I? I mean, you've just saved me from having to run out on another check. I think this is the last place in Los Angeles I haven't done that.'

'I've only been here eight weeks. I've hardly run out on any.'

Her face lit up. 'Oh, it's the best thing!' she insisted. 'You see, it's redistribution of scarce resources.'

'Failing to pay a lunch check is redistribution of scarce resources?'

'I was told that it was. By a . . .' She silently mouthed the final word: *Communist*.

Ken had met one or two in college. They were very serious young men, intent on growing beards and talking about the Soviet miracle. They hadn't been great company.

'Did he also run out on checks?' he asked.

'No, he had family money.' The conversation lulled because there didn't seem an easy reply, so Ken drew the now-useless *Siege of Downville* script from inside his jacket and placed it on the table. She looked down at it and grinned. 'You're an actor!'

'Kinda.' There was a pause and he supposed that she was guessing the truth. 'I just had the audition.'

'Did you get the part?'

'Probably not.'

She sat back, a smug expression crowding out everything else on her face. 'You need to know big people. Know them socially. That's how you get on.'

The subtle 'I've-got-the-inside-track, you-haven't' tone needled him, especially since he was standing her coffee. But during his brief time in LA he had come to understand this was the default position when talking to strangers – a kind of duel for prominence, like two alley cats meeting beside a garbage pail and fighting for its contents.

'Clearly,' he said.

'Do you want to?'

'I . . .'

'Because I can do it. I can.' She leaned forward and rushed on. 'I'm going to a beach party tomorrow. It's at Oliver Tooke's house.' She waited for a reaction. 'The writer?'

Truth be told, the name had rung a distant bell with Ken, but he didn't want to hazard an opinion just yet. 'Okay,' he said, without committing himself.

'At least, I expect he's having a party tomorrow. He does most days. I'll be your ticket in.'

Oliver Tooke. Oliver Tooke. Oh, yes. Yes, now he remembered hearing the name on the radio, a book review programme. But he couldn't recall what the book was about or what opinion the presenter had come up with. 'So you know him?'

'I've met him,' she said proudly.

'Often?'

'We've been introduced at a nightclub.'

Friendship was cheap in this city. He looked down at the script. There were breadcrumbs underneath it. 'I'll come,' he said.

'My name's Gloria.'

'I'm Ken.'

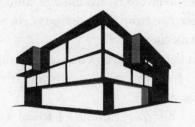

Chapter 2

The next morning, he met Gloria outside her apartment. She had a bundle containing a towel and swimsuit in her arms, tied up with ribbon. She was wearing a sea-green kaftan and a blouse and baggy pants of the same hue. Single-colour ensembles were her look.

'So that people always remember you?' Ken suggested, pointing to her get-up.

'You should try it. You need a look for your career.'

Painful as the thought was, he wondered if, at some point in the future, he really would have to have a 'look'. If he could typecast himself – maybe he could use his small-town background and present himself for cornball parts – it would be a foot in the door. He wasn't going to claim his granddaddy was a Cherokee Indian, but if there was a part for a farm boy from Georgia he would happily turn up in cowpoke boots and drawl his vowels long enough to fit whole sentences in the gaps. It might work, so long as they overlooked his college education and love of British literature from the previous century.

'Which way's the party?'

'The beach behind Oliver's house,' she said. It was just 'Oliver' now. 'Jeez, that place sends me! It's up the coast, so we gotta take a cab.'

He clamped his own bundle of towel and swimming shorts under his arm and felt for his wallet. There was a lot of room in it. 'It had better be less than five bucks there and back or we're walking home,' he told her.

'Don't worry about getting back,' Gloria instructed him. 'Someone will give us a ride. They always do.' She waved at a passing taxi and it stopped so sharply the car behind had to swerve into the neighbouring lane. Its driver thumped the horn. 'Point Dume,' Gloria told the cabbie as they jumped in.

'So, what's he like?' Ken asked.

'Oliver?'

'Yeah, Oliver.'

She considered. 'He's a phony,' she said as they pulled into the traffic. 'I don't like him.'

Her calling Oliver a phony was a level of irony. 'Phony how?'

'Oh, he says things but you know he means something else. That kind of phony.'

'Oh, that kind of phony.'

*

16

Forty minutes later, the driver turned off the coastal high-way and took a road so thin it wouldn't even have been ink on a map. It led up to a promontory of land piercing the Pacific Ocean. The headland that was Point Dume rose up like an arching lizard and there was something reptile-like about its surface too: green, scaly and carnivorous. If you stood there staring into the waves that hid more sharp-toothed creatures, civilization must have seemed far behind you.

There was only one specimen of life on the headland: a large three-storey house, built, by its looks, around the turn of the century. It sat on a low cliff, but what really set it apart was that it seemed to be made almost entirely of glass. The exterior walls were glass, the interior walls were glass. The doors were glass framed by a few splinters of wood. You could walk up from the highway and stare right through it, out to the ocean. Only smoked panes on the upper level prevented you looking right through there too. On top of the house was a weather vane, also made of glass, in the shape of an hourglass. It was twisting in a light breeze like it was pointing the way and the way kept changing. The building was an extraordinary sight, but somehow also wrong, Ken thought. There was just something *off* about its character.

'So this is modern architecture,' Ken said.

'What? No, this is Oliver's house,' Gloria replied. There was little he could think of by way of an answer to that. She stared at him for a moment. 'You're not going to say anything stupid and embarrass me, are you? This is *Oliver*

Tooke we're talking about. There'll be producers here, directors.'

'I'll try not to.' It was becoming pretty clear that they were not suited. He had, at first, held rough ideas of her becoming his girlfriend, and she was an attractive girl, but they were not of one mind. There was an electric bell button beside the front door, and above it hung a steel name sign for the property: Turnglass House. 'Do we ring this?' Ken asked.

'No, they'll all be on the beach.'

She led him around to the back. The earth became more parched as they rounded the building, coming to a garden with a wide slope that led down to the house's private beach, shaped like a waning moon. Ken was used to open horizons. He had grown up camping before them. But he had never, not even in Boston, lived by the sea. It moved and heaved and boomed, whether anyone was listening or not. He understood why some people could never bring themselves to leave it.

The beach was alive with around thirty young people in bathing costumes: some on deckchairs, others splashing about in the surf. The score to the scene came from a hot jazz quartet.

'Can you see him?' Gloria asked.

'I don't know what he looks like.'

'Oh, no, I guess you don't.' There was a drinks station, where staff in sky-blue uniforms were doling out cocktails and fruit. It sure looked like anyone could come in and claim the booze. She searched the scene. 'Where *is* he?' She stopped a girl walking past wearing a pink two-piece costume. 'Where's Oliver?'

'Oh, honey, I'm so wasted, I don't know where *I* am,' the girl burbled.

Ken took that as an invitation to slink over to the drinks table. 'What's everyone drinking here?' he asked the bartender.

'Everyone's drinking a Tom Collins, sir.'

'Then I'll have a Tom Collins.' The barman handed him the drink. 'Where's our host?' The man pointed to the sea. A hundred yards out, Ken could make out something in the waves. It was a strange sight: a whitewashed structure in the water, built like a lighthouse on a rock poking up through the ocean. It looked a few yards wide and a bit taller. He checked back. Gloria had inserted herself into a group of young things screeching with laughter. He wasn't grabbed by the idea of joining them. But their absentee host, Oliver Tooke, well, he sounded like a man worth meeting. So Ken closed himself inside a wooden changing hut and emerged a minute later in striped bathing shorts.

'Ken!' Gloria called after him, but he pretended not to hear and ran headlong into the surf. There had been enough rivers and creeks around his home town to make him a strong swimmer and he powered through the waves, enjoying the sting of salt in his eyes and mouth, and the chance to use his muscles, which had been wasting away in LA. It was a beautiful day and this was a beautiful chunk of coastline. As he swam, he almost lost himself in his dreams. Right up until the second that the rip tide grabbed him.

The moment he swam into its reach, he felt a funnel

of water dragging him at speed straight out to the open sea. The current was stronger than an ox. But with all the effort he had, he managed to swim parallel to the beach, all the while being sucked towards the empty ocean, and after twenty yards of swimming as hard as he could, he felt the current suddenly return to normal. He trod water as he got his breath back until a mechanical hum made him look up and he saw a red speedboat approaching him. The pilot wore the same uniform as the wait staff. The motor died down as it drifted close to him and he caught on to the short ladder on the side, hauling himself up.

'Rip tide, sir,' the young pilot said. 'Comes on without warning. Very dangerous. Are you going to the writing tower?'

Ken glanced at the miniature lighthouse. 'I guess I am.'

The young man pushed the lever forward and they took off towards the whitewashed structure. As they neared it, Ken saw a man standing in a narrow doorway, leaning against the frame, his hands in the pockets of white slacks. He was tall and slim, with narrow features and slicked-down dark hair. He wasn't going to win any beauty pageants, but somehow you would always remember him.

As the boat closed in, the pilot threw the man a line. There was a tiny jetty, no more than a yard across, and Ken stepped onto it.

Up close, he could see that the building was roughly square, built of cubes of stone and about twelve feet wide and twenty high – a little larger than it had appeared from the shore. Its base was uneven, clambering over big dark rocks, and there was a ring of windows around the top,

which made it look even more like a lighthouse squeezed
down by time.

'Howdy,' said the man in the white pants. He didn't
seem at all surprised by the arrival.

'Hi.' Ken wiped his hair back, pressing some of the
brine from it.

'Come on in.'

'Thank you.'

Even though he went in with no expectations, Ken was
still surprised when he stepped into the narrow building.
No lighthouse, it was a shrunken library, kind of like the
one at his college where he had pored over old novels.
Dusty spears of light burst down through windows with
a fine layer of salt on them, illuminating a thousand
volumes clinging to the shelves as if they were afraid of
the water.

'This is incredible,' Ken said.

'This?' The man sounded quite surprised himself and
gazed around as if the strangeness of the place had only
just struck him. 'I suppose it is.' He extended a hand. It
had a white signet ring on the pinkie finger. 'My grandfather built it – along with the house – but I made it my
own. I'm Oliver Tooke.'

'Ken Kourian,' he said, shaking the hand. It was cool
to the touch, as if the man's blood temperature were half
a degree lower than everyone else's.

Oliver's brow furrowed a little. 'Kourian, that a
Yiddisher name?'

'Armenian.'

'Armenian?' The furrow deepened. *'K'ez dur e galis*

im tuny?' His expression said that he hoped he had the pronunciation correct.

Ken laughed. 'That, sir, is incredible. I've never met anyone who spoke a word of the language before.'

'I know a couple of Armenians,' Oliver said, as if that explained why he could speak it.

'Well, since you ask about the house . . .' Ken turned to face where the glass building sat bird-like on the low cliff. 'It's . . .' he hesitated.

'. . . grotesque?' Oliver suggested. The man was direct, there was no doubting that.

'I wouldn't say that.'

'Wouldn't you?' Oliver leaned against a bookcase. His tone was light, as if this was a subject he had thought much about and had long ago come to the conclusion. 'Wouldn't you say there's just something ugly about it?'

'Ugly?'

'I've always thought so.'

'How so?'

'Oh, just something corrupt about it. Malign.' He said it as if detailing no more than the year it was built. Ken was curious. Accuracy aside – and it wasn't an *in*accurate assessment of the building – it was a strange reaction to a family home. Could a house itself be corrupt? Well, perhaps it could. Oliver changed the subject, jerking his chin towards the doorway. 'Did you come with anyone?'

'Gloria,' Ken informed him.

'Oh, girl who always dresses monochrome?'

'That's her.'

'I've spoken to her a couple of times. Maybe three, I

forget.' But Ken got the feeling that Oliver Tooke knew exactly how many times he had spoken to anyone. He could probably recite each conversation word for word. There was a short pause. 'You want to look through the books?'

He must have read Ken's mind. 'I do. I'm always fascinated by other people's reading habits.'

'Me too.' Oliver sat in a fiery red leather captain's chair that was positioned in front of a walnut secretary cabinet. On the opposite edge of the room there was a chaise longue. Ken toured the room, drifting his forefinger over the collection. The titles spanned a wide range of topics, from surgical techniques to French poetry to cookery. Ken wondered if anything tied them all together, other than what appeared to be a voracious and generalized curiosity on the part of their owner. Maybe it wasn't healthy to be interested in everything at once. 'Why do you think we're fascinated by that?' Oliver asked.

'I guess you learn a lot more about someone from the books they read than where they spend their vacations or which box they tick on a voting paper.'

Oliver looked like he agreed. 'You're from the South, aren't you?'

'Georgia.' Ken felt self-conscious. The South wasn't always so popular with certain types.

'Okay. But college too.'

'Yes.'

'Where?'

'Boston.'

'Not Cambridge?'

'No, Boston.'

'I'm glad, Ken. I've met Harvard men. Some of the most stupid people I've ever met.'

'I've found that too.' There was another pause and Ken glanced back at the books on the walls.

'You think we're heading for war again?' Oliver asked, with intense seriousness. It was another leap of topic. Ken was sure it wasn't a put-on, though; the man's mind really did rush from one subject to the next.

'With Germany? Hitler seems insane, but another war? I don't know.'

'Insane men make the news. Don't overlook him.'

'I won't.'

'Some people would,' Oliver said. It sounded like he had someone in mind. Then another subject. 'You're new to LA, aren't you? You want to be in the movies?'

Well, it was a common question when half the people on the street were hoping for a few lines in the next production from United Artists. 'Just like every other rube you sit next to at the diner.'

'Probably. I guess you need something that stands out.'

'Like always wearing one colour.'

'That kinda thing.'

Ken took a look at the secretary cabinet. His host was working on something. There was a typewriter with a sheet of paper poking out, a sentence suspended halfway through. 'Did I disturb you?' He pointed to the typewriter, which had 'Remington' emblazoned across the top in gothic gilt script, and below that 'Made in Ilion, New York, USA'. But as he glanced at it, he saw that the paper within wasn't a script or a novel, but a letter. It was addressed to some convent.

Oliver reached over and whipped the sheet out, laying it face-down on the desk. 'Sorry, pal, it's private,' he said.

'Of course.' Ken was embarrassed, like he had been caught with his fingers in the cookie jar. 'I should get back, leave you to your work.'

'That's good of you. My boat will take you over if you don't want to swim this time.' He smiled a little, but the atmosphere was cooler.

'Thanks.' They made their way to the little jetty.

'But come back, won't you? I'm throwing a party Monday next week. Night-time.'

That evening, Ken returned to the lodging house that he shared with six other residents and a widowed French landlady who was always perfectly made-up, morning, noon and night, despite being at least sixty years old.

It was lucky that the building was in California, because his room was exposed to the open air at seven or eight points of broken window, damaged wall and penetrated ceiling. It was there that he ate too, with a tin plate and an old scout lock-knife that he cleaned and stored in his trunk after meals.

Coming in tired, he flopped onto his bed with his fingers knitted behind his skull. He had forgotten to say goodbye to Gloria when he left, so he would call on her the following day to apologize – after all, she had invited him to the party. And it had been an arresting afternoon.

After a short nap, his peace was interrupted by the

sounds of violence from the adjoining room. His neighbours, a couple from Montreal who by turns yelled at each other without mercy in French or attempted to kill each other through their pulverizing actions in bed, had started early that night. It took him a while to work out which of their two hobbies they were letting rip. He was glad to hear that it was the angry screaming and decided to leave them to it, going down to the communal room that was used for smoking in the evening. The landlady was there, tidying up. She smiled warmly at Ken.

'Good evening, Mr Kourian.'

'Good evening, Madame Peche.'

'You have been out with a young lady?' Her English was perfect, but her accent heavy, and he suspected she put it on just a little. She had been in LA since the previous century.

'How did you know?'

She breathed in spectacularly, absorbing a scent. '*Fleurs de Paris*,' she said. 'An *inexpensive* perfume.'

He laughed. So a little bit of Gloria had rubbed off on him after all. 'Nothing gets past you, does it, Madame?'

She shrugged a little, like a French woman in a movie. 'Not when we talk about *parfum*.'

He collected an old magazine – there were always a few hanging around, cast off by previous tenants – and was about to return to his room in the hope that the murderous noise would have abated, when he turned back to her. 'Madame, have you ever heard of a man named Oliver Tooke?'

Her eyebrows lifted. 'Of course. Why?'

He sat in a worn-down leather armchair. 'I met him tonight. But I don't know much about him.'

'You met him? The state Governor?'

'The Governor?' Ken was puzzled. If Oliver Tooke was the state Governor, he was damn young for such an office. And on top of his writing career? 'I don't think it can be. The one I'm talking about is twenty-eight or so.'

'Ah!' A light of recognition glowed in her face. 'You mean the son of the Governor. Oh, that tragic boy.' This only confused him more and he waited for an explanation. 'So long ago. Were you even born then? I don't know.'

'When?' he asked, hoping the shutters would be opened on the conversation sooner or later.

She thought for a moment. 'My grandson had just been born, I think. So probably around twenty-five years ago.'

'I'm twenty-six,' he replied.

She sighed. 'Such a pity.' Then she shook away whatever thought was in her head. He wasn't sure he wanted to know what it was. 'Governor Tooke. It was before he was Governor . . . You see the glass in these windows?' He nodded. 'Made by Tooke Glass, I expect. They made just about every window in California at one time. Rich, oh so very rich. But it counted for nothing, didn't it?'

'Why?'

She smiled sadly. 'Because Oliver Tooke had two sons. One had his name, the other was . . .' She pursed her lips in thought. 'Alexandre, I think. He was the younger one, Alexandre. But he was taken.'

'What do you mean "taken"?'

She hunted for the word, not one she used often. She pronounced it with unease. 'Abducted. Killed.'

'How?'

She shrugged again. 'I can't remember. So long ago. You met Governor Tooke?' She sounded surprised.

'No,' he said. 'I met the son.'

'Oh, yes.' She tutted at her forgetfulness. 'You met the son. The one who survived.'

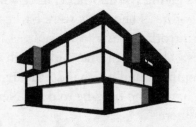

Chapter 3

The next morning Ken was at his desk at eight, sweating over an advert for a soap that claimed to stop men sweating. But the German-sounding client had demanded that words such as 'perspire', 'damp', 'moist' and certainly 'sweat' itself were *verboten*. Ken had to find a way to say something, without using any of the words necessary to convey the meaning. He fixed on the word 'glow' as a code word that might – just – get the message across. The tinkling of a telephone across the room barely registered until his boss, a New York advertising man who had come out west for the sun, hollered over.

'Ken. Phone.'

Ken hauled himself away from the work and lifted the

heavy receiver. He rarely received calls and the heat and frustration with his work had sapped most of his energy. 'Ken Kourian,' he said.

'Ken. *Siege of Downville*. Your screen test was the pits, but someone's giving you another chance. Get here within two hours. Got it?' The words were barked out without any name or introduction.

'Great. Yes. Thank you,' he said, taken aback. There was the thumping sound of a handset being dumped into the cradle. 'I have to go out,' he told the New Yorker.

'Go out? Where?'

'Paramount,' he replied.

'You an advertising man or an actor, Ken?'

'Probably neither,' he replied.

An hour later, he was back in the room where he had had his audition. The assistant producer was watching Ken like you would watch a monkey playing with gasoline and a match. Finally, he spoke. 'You got friends, son?'

'I don't know what you mean.'

'Friends, son. In the business. You must have to be back here.'

'Not that I know of.' He wracked his brains. Unless . . .

'Got a call this morning. Six in the morning. Now, that don't bother me – I'm up at five. Best time of the day. But still – early for a work call. I hear from the producer that some buddy of someone else met some young actor who would be good in one of the small parts.' Ken was about to say something. 'Only it's not such a small part now. Now he's gonna have thirty-something lines. We're getting the rewrite this afternoon. Ring any bells?'

Ken sat back in his seat. This was welcome news: he had a big-shot friend in the industry, something that twenty-four hours earlier had seemed a slim hope.

'I don't even want to know. Well, Wardrobe need to see you. Get down there. You're a Union officer.'

'Union? But I'm from Georgia.'

'That's what I damn well told them.'

He was to play a lieutenant who was the voice of reason next to his bloodthirsty senior officers, which meant that for the next five days Ken spent his lunch breaks in costume fittings and learning his lines. And then when the day came – it was to be an exhausting spin of the earth, because it was also to be the day of Oliver's party – he was ready, waiting in front of his boarding house, only for a runny-nosed messenger boy to turn up and tell him that shooting had been put back for twenty-four hours and he should kick back at home after all.

Knocked out by the nerves and subsequent letdown, he went back to bed. It was a waste of a day booked off from the office but, well, at least he could rest up for the party that evening. Gloria had gotten in touch to tell him they would be going together again and he should pick her up in a taxi. Her voice sounded put out when she asked him why he had abandoned her last time. He made up some need to be back at his lodging by a certain time or the door would have been locked. It sounded hollow because it was.

'Well, this time you're seeing me home,' she said.

31

'Okay.' He hoped that that meant only as much as its literal meaning.

A stream of cars stopped one by one in front of Oliver's house while jazz soaked the night air. Ken breathed it in, thrilled that this could be his first real movie party, the type written about in the *Los Angeles Times* gossip column: skin against skin, dope and scandal.

Gloria was wearing a short dress decked out with more scarlet feathers than an Amazonian parrot. She dusted down Ken's one good suit as they passed through a black-and-white tiled hallway, past a wide wooden staircase that led upstairs – which, it seemed, was a single double-height storey – into what was described as 'the ballroom'. The spacious chamber was decked with white marble, and at one side a white baby grand piano was in high demand. Whoever was playing knew his way around a keyboard like a surgeon knows his way around a pair of tonsils.

The corner opposite was given over to an indoor sunken pool, where a number of bathing beauties had taken the hint and were submerged in what could have been swimming costumes or just their underclothes. Some didn't appear to be wearing even those.

All around the room, bodies were crowded together: dancing, cooing at each other, bickering. And despite her demand that Ken see her home tonight, in less than five seconds Gloria had spotted some friends and left him at the bar. He really didn't mind.

Looking around, he noted that beside the rows of brightly coloured bottles of whiskey, gin and vermouth, all eager soldiers to the fight, there were small covered silver platters. He lifted the lid from one. It exposed a short line of white powder with a metal straw beside it. He put the lid back. He had been offered cocaine in college and he hadn't wanted it then and didn't want it now. If his fellow guests felt like getting screwy that night, that was their business.

He took a drink – this time everyone was downing martinis with molehills of blackberries stuffed into them – and scanned the place. Outside, he spotted the man he was looking for, drifting down the slope to the beach. Ken pushed through the crowd, but when he reached the garden, Oliver had disappeared.

'Ken! Come here!' It was Gloria. She beckoned him over to where she sat on a linen-covered couch, draped over a man who would have been handsome if it weren't for his cheeks running to jowls and eyes so bloodshot Ken could have seen them at ten paces. 'Ken Kourian, this is Piers Bellen. He's a producer at Warner.' She winked in a manner that she seemed to think was subtle.

'Pleased to . . .'

'I need to powder my nose,' she said, rubbing it in a manner that suggested she wasn't going to the ladies' room to do it. 'But don't let him get away.'

She flitted up, leaving Ken with the man. He was perspiring – or 'glowing' as the *Times* advert would have it – right through a shirt, tie, vest and suit jacket.

'How are you, Mr Bellen?'

'Pissed,' he grumbled.

Ken guessed this was not going to be an easy conversation. 'Any special reason?'

'Fucking Code meeting today.'

'I'm sorry?' He had an idea what the man meant, but he had already decided not to help him out.

Bellen grumbled on. 'Hays Code. It's coming down hard. That man wants to bankrupt us all. What, no sex on the screen? No blaspheming? No rape? What the hell are we going to show? Congress has no idea what we con'ribute to this nation.'

Ken decided he was all in now. 'And what do you contribute?' he asked.

'Dreams. Fucking dreams. Cornball like you should 'ppreciate that.' Well, the insult would have cut deeper if Ken hadn't been sure that Bellen had far less education than him. 'Why the hell else d'you come here? Why didn't you stay down on the farm?'

'I didn't grow up on one.' He had, really, but he also enjoyed lying to people like Bellen.

Bellen wasn't defeated, however. 'Sure. But you know plenty who did. This country? It's a fucking dream. What'd that Jewess write on the Statue of Liberty? "Give me your huddled masses yearning to be free"? You know what yearning means?'

'I know what it m—'

'It means dreaming. They need dreams. We give them dreams. For ten cents. For ten fucking cents, they can dream they're flying to Mexico or eating fifteen courses or screwing Greta Garbo. Hunger? Bills to pay? Not here. None here. They're all 'tside the theatre. That's why they need us. You gotta problem with that?'

'Several,' he said. He wasn't angry, he was just tired by

the conversation, even though it had been raging for less than a minute.

'Then you should—'

'I should nothing.'

'What? You—'

'Look, I've been with you thirty seconds and that's enough for anyone. I'm going to the cocktail counter. I'd ask you what you want, but I don't care.' He heaved himself to his feet and fought his way back into the house.

'You told Bellen where to get off.'

Oliver had appeared with a coupette in his hand. It was swimming with a light brown liquid and ice.

Ken sighed. 'You think it wasn't a smart move. A producer and all that.'

Oliver sipped his drink. 'He's still telling people that?'

So, the man was a fraud as well as a farmyard animal. 'What is he really?'

Oliver put his hand through the crook of Ken's arm and steered him back down to the shoreline. 'A clerk.'

'Who for?'

Oliver hesitated, as if considering whether to reveal something quite secret. 'I forget,' he said.

Well, Ken believed that as much as he believed a seven-dollar bill. But Oliver would tell him if and when he was ready. And there was something Ken wanted to bring up as they looked out on the surf rolling in like white tigers. 'I got a call from Paramount last week.'

'Oh yes?'

'They've given me a part in a film. Someone recommended me.' There was no answer. 'Thanks.'

'Don't mention it.'

'I will, though. This is a big thing for me.'

Oliver wandered over to a nearby drinks table and came back having swapped his coupette for a bottle of Crémant and two flute glasses. He twisted away the wire and let the cork blast itself free. Some of the wine fizzed down the neck of the bottle. 'You seem a good guy, Ken. So I did what I could and I hope it leads to bigger things.'

'It might.' He rarely allowed himself to dream. But he liked where the future was pointing.

Oliver hesitated for a moment, then looked out to the ocean and waved. At his signal, the little launch steered away from its course tracing figure-eights in the sea and came to rest a few yards out from the dry sand. 'It's quite the sunset tonight,' Oliver said, gazing out. They waded through the rippling water and jumped into the boat, which spun around and bumped over waves tinted orange by the setting sun. 'Maybe I should write a movie for you to star in,' Oliver yelled over the roar of the engine as they approached the writing tower.

'I think that would be asking a lot.'

'I've never written a movie. There's more money in books. For now.'

'How important is money?'

'I grew up with it, pal. I'm addicted to it. You take it away from me and I'll collapse in on myself.'

This was a surprising thing to say. Sure, money had been tight in Ken's youth – deathly tight in those hungry years they called a Depression – but he had always presumed that those who had money and had always had it looked upon it with carelessness. 'You must have enough, though.'

'No such thing to an addict. That's what addiction means. More drink, more junk. However much you have, you need more.'

'So why not just stay in the family business? Glass, right?'

'Glass, yes. Built this place. Well, I'm probably better for the firm staying away from it. As it is, it keeps rolling out the panes and rolling in the dollars. And so, I have time to write.'

The boat dropped them on the rocky outpost of the Tooke family estate and they entered. Oliver lit an oil lamp overhead that hissed into life, throwing a hot glow over the books. 'I've been working on something new,' he said. 'Something I . . .' He stopped, losing his thought midway through.

'What is it?' Ken prompted him.

Oliver snapped back into the room and went to the secretary cabinet. He took a thin key and unlocked it to reveal a short stack of books. Some were dog-eared modern paperbacks – the type of trash that private school kids would hide from their teachers – others looked quite holy, bound in flaking leather.

He took one from the stack that turned out to be a dime-novel. *He Wanted Her Dead* blazed a lurid cover decked out with a gumshoe pointing his .45 revolver down an alleyway. On the ground was a blond girl with her skirt hiked up her thigh.

'What do you think it's about?' Oliver asked.

'I guess a private dick who . . .' He began to open the

book. But Oliver plucked it from his grip, flipped it over and thrust it back into Ken's hand.

'What about now?' Ken looked down, expecting to see a ham-fisted description of the plot and the character of the tough-guy protagonist. Instead, he found another book altogether. *She Needed to Kill* screamed this one. And the gun this time was a little Derringer in the palm of the same blonde, now upright and pointing the pistol at the detective's back. Ken was struck by the book being two, and turned it over to gaze at the first cover again. 'The format is ... gripping, isn't it?' Oliver said. 'One story and then turn it over and it's another, but a sort of mirror image of the first. Maybe the characters look very different from a different point of view.'

'I guess so.'

'It's what I've been working on. In a way. People changing from one viewpoint to another. One year to another.' He stared through the doorway at the black waves lapping on the rocks. 'People do change.' His voice had a thoughtful, faraway quality.

'Oh, not that much.'

'You think?' Oliver paused for a moment, apparently lost in his own thoughts, before continuing. 'When I was very young, I was in a wheelchair – polio, a bad case. I'm told I had to be strapped into it or I'd fall out. I'm fine now, my body adapted and grew.'

'That's good.' Ken had the impression there was more to what Oliver was saying than he was actually saying. He waved the book. 'Did you write this?'

'This one? No, someone else.'

'What do you call them? Books like this?'

'*Tête-bêche* is the term. Head to foot. They're pretty old as an idea – this is how they used to be.' He picked the top volume from the pile and handed it to Ken. The cracking chestnut-coloured leather binding was inlaid with gold letters that were mostly rubbed away but still decipherable. The front was the New Testament with script so tiny that just reading it brought on a headache. Turned over, it was a book of psalms. 'A bit more religious than what they became.'

'That's for sure.' Ken held it next to *He Wanted Her Dead*.

'Gizmo for publishers now. Buy one book, get two! Of course, it doesn't mean that when you think about it – you're getting the same number of pages.' He tidied a few items on his desk that had become disordered.

'I'd like to read this,' Ken told him, flicking through the detective novel.

'Be my guest, pal. In fact, take any of them you like.' He jerked a thumb at the deck of books.

Ken noticed something a little different at the bottom of the pile, a white notebook. He drew it out. The front bore the handwritten name *The Turnglass* – it wouldn't sell so well on the newsstands as *She Needed to Kill*. Ken didn't know all that much about Oliver Tooke's work, but surely detective pulp was a bit of a change of direction? Well, perhaps he wanted to try something new.

He opened the front page. 'Simeon Lee's grey eyes were visible . . .' it began.

But Oliver's hand interrupted and gently closed the book. 'I'm still working on it,' he said. 'I don't quite know how it ends yet.' Ken let him take it back and return it to the bottom of the pile. He locked the cabinet again.

'You know the beginning, though.'

'Sure. But the ending's far more important,' Oliver replied. 'It'll be published soon. You can read it then.'

'How can it be if you don't know the ending?'

'Well, I do and I don't. Anyhow, come the end of June, it's in the shops.'

That was pretty soon if Oliver hadn't finished writing it. Ken guessed the publishing schedules for this kind of pulp novel were short. 'So it's like the others, you flip it over and get another story?'

'It is, but I've only written one of them. The publisher's got someone else to do the other – something they think will fit with mine. One day, though, I'm going to write my own companion piece. The same story but from a different direction. Its reflection.'

'You know, I could read it before it's out,' Ken said, pointing at the secretary cabinet. 'Jemmy the lock, break my way in.'

'You could,' Oliver conceded. 'But you won't.'

'Tell me why.'

Oliver thrust his hands in his pockets. 'Because you're too respectful of right and wrong. And I think that's what I need more of around here. Anyhow, you don't have long to wait.'

'True.' Now that his vision had adjusted to the low light in the room, Ken spotted something unexpected tucked away at the side. It was an easel, with a painting on it covered with a sheet. 'You have a hobby.'

'I find it clears my head.' He sounded almost apologetic. 'To tell you the truth, pal, I find parties pretty exhausting and I like to come out here for a while when they're on. People don't seem to miss me when the bash is in full swing.'

'I can understand that. About parties, I mean. The host has the hardest job of all.'

'I kinda fell into that role.' It was obvious that Oliver wasn't totally happy that he had done so.

Ken could picture him discreetly calling his launch, setting out over the waves and spending a half hour at his canvas or his typewriter – ready to set the party smile back in place and head into the battleground spilling out of his house. 'May I?' he asked as he went to the picture.

'Be my guest.'

Ken lifted the cover and found a medium-sized painting. It was in the early stages, with more pencil lines than paint, ready to guide the artist's brush. But it seemed to be a portrait of a woman in front of the glass house on the cliff.

'Who is she?'

'No one in particular.'

Ken pondered if that could be true. Artists – even amateur artists – never just painted random figures, they always had someone in mind. So he wondered still who she was.

The rest of the party passed in a haze of singing, bathing and people yelling themselves hoarse above the din. Ken took the chance to explore the house a little. Upstairs had five bedrooms, a library and a couple of bathrooms. All had doors made of opaque smoked glass, coloured red, green or blue. Sometime after midnight, Gloria appeared in the ballroom with a silver tray striped with white powder. She insisted Ken try some and he resisted with equal force until she gave up, pouting her lips and calling him a dull son-of-a-bitch and he had better remember he was taking her home tonight or she would make him sorry. And then, half an hour later, she told him that Piers Bellen – 'the producer from Warner that you were so rude to' – was going to see her home, but he had kindly agreed to give Ken a ride even though his rudeness had been totally uncalled for. Ken was so tired by that point that he agreed.

Bellen was already in the driving seat when Ken got into the rear of a tiny white European car. His seat was more suited to a lapdog than a human, and as he eased himself down, Ken saw Bellen's eyes. Even in the glimmers from the house, he could tell the pupils were shrunken, and there were two rough smudges of white under his nostrils. He prayed they would get home – or at least somewhere close – without driving off the road.

'I'm thirsty. And hungry,' Bellen shouted as the ocean road whipped past them.

'Sorry to hear that,' Ken replied with irony that was lost on its subject, but not on Gloria, who glared at him.

'Want a hamburger.' They were passing a billboard advertising meat. 'And Coke.'

'Don't you think you've had enough of that?!' Gloria laughed. But Bellen's face only registered confusion.

'What?'

'I mean, like, white coke. Powder. You know: junk.'

'Oh!' His face cracked into a smile and he guffawed too as he pressed on the accelerator, speeding them even faster and less steadily along the road. But then he suddenly slammed on the brakes.

'Christ!' Ken gasped as he cannoned into the back of Gloria's seat.

'There it is!' Bellen said, pointing and spinning the wheel so that they turned into the parking lot of an all-night grill.

He dragged up the hand brake and ran towards the entrance. Ken and Gloria had no choice but to follow. As Bellen kicked open the chrome door, he turned back to them. His face was curdling as if he had sucked on a lemon. 'Shines,' he called loudly.

'What?' Ken replied.

Bellen pointed to a coloured man and his girl approaching the 'to go' counter.

'Shines. Everywhere.' He made sure the whole room could hear him. For sure the black man could, and gave him a hard look before going back to his conversation with the waitress.

'I said, shines everywhere!' This time, he bawled it.

'Oh, Jesus Christ,' Ken said to himself. He wanted to leave, but they were miles from anywhere and the only transport was Piers Bellen.

And then Bellen changed up a gear. 'We white. You negro. You wait!' He was growling in a fake tribal voice, thrusting a sweaty arm between the couple and the counter.

The coloured man glared at him, then replied, 'We here first. You after.' And he pushed the arm away with the same force. But the man couldn't know what Bellen had been snorting and how it was affecting his brain. Suddenly Bellen's fist – heavy though unpractised, judging by its swinging haymaker – was connecting with dark brown flesh, and a slimmer elbow was thudding into Bellen's solar plexus in return and the waitress was calling the cops and Gloria was screaming her head off and Ken was wishing to God he had found another way home.

Two hours later, Ken sat, drenched in the sweat of night, on a bench in University Avenue police precinct house, three paper cups stained with coffee dregs at his feet. The other couple had been interviewed, processed and bounced. Bellen was at the payphone shouting again.

'Fucking shine hit me, Tooke. A fucking ... They're uppity now. I swear, they should never have been set free. He fucking smacked me one, you hear?' There was a short silence, as Oliver Tooke presumably got a few words in. 'Isn't it obvious, you numbskull? You come down here and bail me. Fucking police bail.' Another few seconds of calm. And then Bellen lowered his voice to a threatening hiss. 'Because if you don't, then you don't get what I've found out for you. You'll never know what happened.' And, bizarre as it sounded, he put on a high-pitched, wheedling female voice. 'Oh, Ollie, little Ollie. What really happened to me?' He reverted to his previous hiss. 'Only you won't be able to do nothing because you don't know what happened.' And he slammed down the receiver. A rictus grin was affixed to his mouth as he strode over to where Ken and Gloria sat wilting on the bench. 'Tooke'll come. In twenty fucking minutes.'

And the strange thing, to Ken's mind, was that Tooke came. In twenty fucking minutes.

Chapter 4

Ken had a 6am call for some establishing shots for *The Siege of Downville* and had booked another day off from work at the newspaper. That had given him a full two hours' sleep. As the film crew's wristwatches ticked past nine and he sat baking in full costume, waiting to walk past in a group scene, his mind buzzed with questions as to why the hell Oliver would drive from his house in the middle of the night and hand two hundred dollars to the Los Angeles police department to spring a lying boor like Piers Bellen. And whatever the answers, he had a sinking feeling that that lost night might have spelled the end of his friendship with Oliver Tooke.

His mind pounding with the heat, lack of sleep and

the dregs of martinis kicking at the inside of his skull, he dragged himself over to the second assistant director. 'I'm real sorry, but could I go somewhere cool to wait?' he asked.

The young man tried to place him. 'Lieutenant Brooks, right?'

'Yes,' Ken nodded enthusiastically. It was about the first time anyone had recognized him or his part.

'Take your pick. There's the bench over there in the sun, or there's the trailer. It's made outta steel and it's like being in an oven. Take your shitty pick.' And he checked a clipboard with a thick ream of sheets before walking away. Ken went to the bench.

The sun was pummelling down like he had offended it. It scratched at his face and somehow forced its way through the fabric to burn him through his clothes. When he stood up, unable to take it any more, he could feel the skin on his chest crackle. Could the trailer be any worse? He pulled himself over to it, to find twenty extras and a couple of main cast members crowding into its shadow. 'Whatever you do, sport, don't even think of getting in there,' one young man rasped at him. 'You won't come out again.'

Ken squirmed himself between a coloured girl playing a brilliant and dangerous spy for the Union and a one-handed man appearing as a storekeeper. The man had already filmed his only scene, where he got shot in the crossfire between the two armies, but had been told to hang around indefinitely just in case they wanted to bring him back. 'Bring me back? I get killed in the first minute!'

he was complaining. 'What kinda doctors they have back then? Witch doctors?'

'That's lunch, everyone!', shouted through a metal cone by a kid who looked like he was excited to be out of his high-school math lesson, were the most popular words of the day. While Ken made his way through a plate of bread and Mexican beans with some unidentifiable meat sausage on the side, he caught sight of the director – an effusive and very short man with a moustache that would have suited nobody on earth – coming out of a trailer, followed a minute later by a red-headed actress who had been cast in a small part. Ken was not one bit surprised when word got round an hour later that the leading lady, who had been found doped out on the floor of her bathroom, was being replaced by the redhead.

'Fun and games, don't ya think?' said one of the older women.

'I guess so.'

'This your first one of these?'

'My first.'

'I've done three in the last month. It's exploitation.'

'It is?'

'I've done Shakespeare. Now this.' She waved her hand to indicate everything. 'Just exploitation.'

They were interrupted by the third assistant director grabbing Ken and marching him over to a scene that was just starting up. 'You're in this one,' he was told.

'Am I? It's not in the script.'

'You're working from the wrong draft. You're on the green. We're on yellow now,' he said, flapping the sheaf of yellow pages in Ken's chest.

'Okay. Do I have lines?'

'Right here.' He pointed some out.

'That's not me,' Ken said, disappointed.

'What?'

'I'm Lieutenant Brooks.'

They both stared at the lines ascribed to another character. 'Ah, shit,' the man grumbled, and he left to find the right actor.

Somehow Ken made it through the day, getting back to his lodging house just after five. By that point, he had walked once up a hill while the cameras pointed in another direction. When he arrived home, he found a note pushed under his door. It was in the olde-worlde hand of his landlady.

'Mr Kourian. Mr Tooke called by. He said that he was sorry for any inconvenience last night and hopes that you are quite well. He would like to invite you to dinner at the Plaza Hotel Friday evening at eight. He has a very nice car.' The last statement was, he was sure, her own thought, rather than Oliver's.

He placed the slip of good-quality writing paper on his bedside table, took off his shoes and jacket and fell asleep in his clothes.

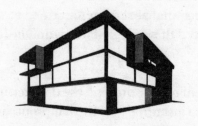

Chapter 5

Over the next few weeks, he saw Oliver a number of times. They would often go to dinner at upmarket restaurants where Oliver would discreetly add the bill to his personal account. In return, Ken would buy them hot dogs from carts at lunchtime. It worked.

'Isn't it tomorrow that your book comes out? The upside-down one?' Ken asked one night. He was yelling because they had ringside seats at a boxing fixture and the crowd was louder than an express train.

Oliver took a while to answer. '*The Turnglass.* Yes.'

The fighter in gold trunks broke out with a vicious upper cut, sending his opponent in black trunks sprawling. The crowd leaped to their feet, baying for blood.

'So you're happy with the ending now?'

'I wouldn't ...' Oliver trailed off. He was usually so precise with his words. 'Maybe. I guess so.'

'Will you tell me what it's about?'

Oliver hesitated before answering. 'Did I mention, my father's family are from England?'

'No.'

'They are. From a county on the east coast. Essex. That's where the family seat is – our house here is a copy of it, only made out of glass. We used to visit the old place sometimes – it's on a tiny island called Ray. All quite desolate. I've set the book there.'

'Interesting. And what's the story like?'

Oliver was quiet for a while again before he answered. 'It's a sad story.' He didn't often speak emotionally, not like that. He was normally matter-of-fact.

'Will readers buy that?'

The match crowd howled as the black-trunked boxer, charging back from the rope, opened up a wide cut on his opponent's cheek. 'Lots of them,' Oliver told him.

'So who's going to be sad about it?'

'I am.'

At the sound of an urgent brass bell, the fight ended with the gold trunks declared the winner. The victory seemed to put a halt on the conversation and they went out to eat at a place Oliver knew that opened late, then took a walk along Sunset in the cooler air, enveloped by chirping crickets and gasoline fumes. An air of humid desperation was hovering over Los Angeles. Ken felt it, hanging there as the clock ticked to 2am and the drunks and hobos picked through trash heaps.

'Your book'll be out in a few hours,' Ken mentioned, looking at his watch.

'I guess it will.'

'Oliver, I don't know any other authors. But I'm pretty sure most of them are more excited about their new book appearing.'

Oliver stopped and looked back down the street. It was quiet now, no more than a handful of cars winding their way home. 'I'm not sure it's the right thing,' he said.

'Why not?'

'Because of guilt. Because I'm guilty.'

Ken stopped and sat on a concrete bench someone had set beside the road for no reason. 'Guilty of what?'

'Being here,' Oliver replied, remaining standing and gazing down the road.

'Is that really something you can be guilty of? Being alive?'

'Sometimes.'

'That's garbage. So will you tell me what's brought this to your mind right now?'

Oliver seemed to waver. But then he came down on one side. 'Another time.' He made his tone lighter again, as if a part of him, briefly allowed to emerge into the light, had been pushed back inside, and Ken let it drop. Oliver would talk when he was ready.

They walked and spoke about nothing special until

something took their feet along Olympic and they came upon a bookstore with a lit window display. Prominent in it was *The Turnglass*.

'Now let it all come down,' Oliver said, almost to himself.

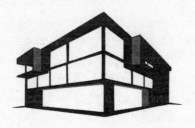

Chapter 6

It was that weekend, the Saturday morning that the calendar marked as the first day of July, that Ken spoke his first and last words in a talking picture. They were immediately forgettable even to him – something about a senior officer being unhappy with arrangements for billeting the regiment, and a subsequent argument about the time the troops had been marching. But the director accepted the delivery without any sign he had even heard them, and because it was an early-morning scene, Ken was back at his digs by ten o'clock. As he walked from the bus stop, he was surprised to see Oliver waiting outside the house, his arms crossed, leaning on the hood of a big car, a Cadillac Phaeton. Ken's landlady had been right when she had praised it.

'Want to meet my father?' Oliver asked as Ken came near.

Up to that point, Ken had only heard about the man, Oliver Tooke Senior, from his landlady and sometimes read about him in the newspapers. 'Why not?'

A chauffeur opened the door and Ken entered. The car purred out into steady traffic. 'Sorry, pal. I forgot. You probably have no idea who my father is. Dad's state Governor,' Oliver explained. Ken didn't say anything. 'He's back from Sacramento. He usually lives in the Governor's residence there, but he's in town for an event and while he's here W2XAB is interviewing him for the nightly news. Dad wants a show of old family strength at the old family home.'

Ken had barely even thought about the fact that Oliver's glass-walled home wasn't actually his – it was his father's, and all the furniture, the books, the piano, all belonged to Governor Tooke.

'What sort of event?' Ken asked.

'It's a political thing. He's going to run for President next year. He should get the Republican nomination, and he's hosting a little soiree for some of the local organizers.'

'So he's canvassing for votes.'

'Votes? Hell no, nothing so tawdry. Dad's canvassing for money.'

The family were wealthy, but the spend for a presidential primary would probably be beyond even their deep pockets.

On the way, Ken thought of the last party he had attended at the Tooke home. The night hadn't ended well; and if Oliver hadn't been able to place his hands on a couple hundred bucks to post bail for Piers Bellen, it might have turned out worse. As they neared the house, he spoke. 'What does Piers Bellen have on you?'

He thought Oliver would have good reason to send him right back home for prying like that, but his friend didn't even look put out. 'I thought you'd ask that sooner or later.'

'Why?'

'Because you're a perceptive man.'

'And what's the answer?'

Oliver glanced at him but didn't reply.

The cruise-liner-sized car swept into the driveway and they sauntered into the house. Something in the lobby caught Ken's attention: above the fireplace was a painting, and he was sure it hadn't been there before. He recognized it as the one he had seen on the easel in the writing tower, now completed. It was a portrait of a woman aged perhaps thirty, with the house pictured in the background. The subject had chestnut brown hair falling across her shoulders and bright eyes – unnaturally bright, truth be told, because they had been pictured with a sunbeam glaring into them. Her clothes were a little out of fashion, that even Ken could tell.

'Is it anyone in particular?'

'You haven't read my book yet, have you?' Oliver's tone was amused admonishment.

'Not yet – the movie shoot got in the way, but I prom- ise I will.'

'Okay. Let's go up.'

They ascended the stairs and walked the length of the landing, opening the green smoked-glass door to the library. Ken had only had a brief look into the room before. It had dark wood-panelled walls and a slow air to it, as if its summer days were long gone and it was facing a bleak winter.

'Sitting with me today is Mr Oliver Tooke, Governor of California,' barked a bald-headed man holding a microphone in his lap. 'Governor, will you please tell the viewers at home what's on your mind as we approach the presidential primaries?'

On the wall above them hung a family portrait. There was the Governor standing with his hand firmly on the shoulder of his seated wife: a man with bearing and steel-grey hair, a woman with beauty and warm features; and in front of them, their children. But Ken was surprised by two aspects to the picture. The first was that there weren't just the two children Ken's landlady had mentioned, but three: two boys under the age of five and looking like peas in a pod – dark hair framing identical round faces – and a baby held by the mother. One of the boys was in a wheel-chair and Ken remembered that Oliver had said polio had kept him in one as a child.

The other surprise was that the woman in the painting was undoubtedly the subject of the portrait downstairs – the picture that Oliver had claimed was of no one in particular.

'Two words, sir, two words: social corruption,' was the Governor's reply. Ken heard a voice that was almost the same as Oliver's, only aged by time and by heavy smoking that had also turned the Governor's teeth the colour of wheat. 'And I'm sorry to say that a major source of it is the motion picture industry right here in California. Now, I'm a big fan of the talkies myself, but we have a lot of young folk going these days and they're seeing a lot of things they oughtn't.'

'What sort of thing?'

Here we go, Ken thought to himself. Sodom and Gomorrah downtown. Politicians were filling newspaper page after newspaper page with their condemnation.

'Well, they're seeing narcotic use and they're seeing brutal violence and they're copying it. Why wouldn't they when it all looks so sharp on the screen?'

'Countering violent crime is Dad's big thing,' Oliver whispered.

'So I see. It looks genuine.'

'It's personal.'

'How so?'

'I had a brother.' Oliver's face showed a mix of emotions: sadness and something that seemed more like anger. 'I was five, Alex was four. He was abducted.'

'From here?'

'Here? Oh, no. We were at our other house. The one in England. We never saw him again.' He gazed out the window. 'I hate that place.'

It was time to confess. 'Someone told me it had happened, actually.'

'Figures.' Oliver shrugged. 'Someone always tells.' He cleared his throat. 'Anyway, Dad's been heavy on crime ever since.'

A producer put his finger to his lips to tell them to shut up.

The interview ended. 'Have you heard what happened to the President today?' the interviewer asked as they stood.

'I heard he fell out of his wheelchair,' Tooke replied with a smirk. 'Elect a cripple, get a cripple. The American people have only got themselves to blame.'

The interviewer snorted with laughter, then proposed they record a little footage outside in the garden. Tooke agreed and the cameras filmed him walking on the clifftop lawn beside his son, with the sea beyond. 'Your grandfather planted these gardenias,' he was saying. 'He knew that if you have good roots, you have a strong plant. Like strong families. Everything that we are stems from him.' It was baloney for the microphones and cameras. And despite the flowers that surrounded them in regimented rows, Ken couldn't help but remember what Oliver had said when he'd first met him: that there was something corrupt and malign about the house.

Nevertheless, they stopped to admire the gardenias. At the end, the camera crew packed up and the Governor asked Oliver if he was still going around with the sodomites in the movie industry.

'Some of them, Dad. Not all.'

'At least they can't breed.'

'I guess not.'

'I want to lead this nation,' Tooke Senior said, stretching out his back. 'It's vital right now with the situation in Europe – the Democrats would take us into another disaster of a war against Germany. For what? To see a million American boys torn to pieces? And you having faggots for tea doesn't help my chances. People will presume I raised one myself.'

'I'll ask them to stop.'

The Governor nodded. At the end of the lawn, there was a wrought iron octagonal summerhouse with a love seat of the same metal at its centre. Sitting there, impassively watching their approach, was a strikingly beautiful woman with dark hair almost to her waist. She wore a white outfit and a wide-brimmed hat that was keeping the sun off her pale face. Her arm was stretched along the top of the seat. A cigarette was burning in her fingers, and as they neared her, she took a drag, then cast it aside and leaned her cheek on her arm.

'Hello, Coraline,' Oliver said. She looked from him to his friend. 'This is Ken Kourian. Ken, my sister, Coraline.'

He extended a hand and she took it. 'You're a friend of my brother's?' she said. Her voice was soft, as if she was in the habit of only speaking to people within arm's length.

'I like to think so.'

She gazed at him as if he had spoken too quietly to hear. Then she turned to her father. 'How much has Fletcher offered you?' she asked.

'Not enough,' he grumbled.

'You'll have to confront him one day.' And then to her brother: 'I think I'll stay here for a while. I'm tired of Sacramento.' Ken would have been lying if he had then denied the existence of a little civil war inside his chest at the prospect of Coraline Tooke living at the house where he had become a regular visitor. 'Are you in the movies?' Coraline asked Ken.

'Trying.'

'You've got that look about you.'

'What sort of look?'

'Soon-to-be-disappointed.'

A butler intervened and told the Governor that the film crew were leaving and the producer wanted a brief word. He followed the servant back to the house.

'Could you show Ken around the garden?' Oliver asked. 'I need to speak to Carmen for a while.'

'Who's Carmen?' Ken asked, unable to hold his curiosity.

'The maid,' Coraline replied. 'Sure, I'll play house.'

Oliver followed in his father's footsteps, and Ken and Coraline spoke for a few minutes without actually saying anything. The garden, the weather. The things strangers say to each other while waiting for a streetcar. Ken's gaze fell on the house's double-height upper storey. The two rows of windows were arched and large, and he saw Oliver framed in one, speaking earnestly to an old Mexican woman who seemed to be in tears. She ran out of sight and Oliver stood looking just like he had taken a punch in the gut.

'Do you ride, Mr Kourian?' Coraline asked.

'I grew up in Georgia, miss,' he said distractedly. 'If I didn't, I wouldn't get anywhere.'

'Good,' she said. 'I've been looking for a hack. We'll ride today.'

*

An hour later, Ken, Oliver and Coraline entered the gates of a livery stable a few miles up the coast. They wore jodhpur pants, Ken having squeezed into an old pair of Oliver's. 'We've kept our horses here as long as I can remember,' Coraline said.

'She was the most competitive girl rider you ever saw,' Oliver muttered. 'Only thing that ever raised her heartbeat above twenty per minute.'

'And he was slower than the ocean,' she said, leading the way around the back. A stable lad ran to bring her the necessary tack. 'Here we go. This is Bedouin. Don't you think he looks like Oliver?'

The horse was a piebald gelding. 'Sure. It's all in the face.'

'Exactly.'

'Thanks, both of you,' Oliver replied. 'I'll be on Ricky there, and you can have Dad's mount, Stetson. Think you can handle a stallion?'

'He grew up in Georgia – if he couldn't ride, he wouldn't get anywhere,' Coraline told him. Ken detected a sardonic lilt in her voice.

'I guess I'm going to have to prove that, aren't I?'

They saddled up and trotted out. Coraline kicked her heels hard into Bedouin's flank even before they were through the gates, cantering down to the beach. The path was a narrow one with loose rocks and it wouldn't have taken much for the horse to miss a step.

'It's keep up or fall behind, pal,' Oliver shouted as he matched his sister's speed. 'I learned that a long time ago with Coraline.'

'I guess it is!' Ken replied, laughing. It had been a few

years, but the thrill of racing along the track with his new friend and the girl with dark hair streaming behind her like ribbons surged. 'How often do you do this?' he yelled as the path met the damp sand and the horses, getting a whiff of a hunt in their nostrils, took it upon themselves to increase to a full gallop.

'Not often enough. Only when Coraline's death-wish overcomes my sense of self-preservation.' And at that, he smacked his heels into his mount's sides, spurring the horse to leave the ground entirely and fly over a thin creek trickling to the sea.

Ken did the same, feeling the joy of belonging as the three of them abandoned all caution. They were all now bound to live or die as one. And the distance between him, Oliver and Coraline began to close inch by inch. The sun was blazing and the sea was foaming and the horses were snorting and then . . . And then nothing at all as the world spun into confusion and chaos and blackness.

'He's not very good at that, is he?'

The voice was coming through the dark. And as he forced his eyelids up, wincing at the light and the banging pain at the back of his skull, shapes seemed to emerge. The voice belonged to someone looking down at him.

'Are you okay, pal?'

A hand reached for him. Instinctively, he grabbed hold of it. 'I feel like I've fallen off a horse,' he mumbled.

'Yeah, you look like it too.'

'I expect the horses are slower in Georgia,' Coraline remarked.

'We breed them that way. For our own safety.' Breathing in was painful. Breathing out was twice as bad. He tried to work out if he had broken anything except his self-respect.

'How about a little bit of sympathy?' Oliver admonished his sister.

'You give it to him. If you can't stay on a horse, you shouldn't get on one.'

'Give the man a break. His saddle came loose.' Oliver lifted Ken to his feet. 'She's always like this.' Ken focused on his horse, whose saddle was hanging off the side. 'You need me to help you home?'

That would have been more painful than falling off the horse. 'I'll be fine.'

'See, big brother? He'll be fine. Stop your fussing.'

'I don't want him to sue you.'

'Sue me?'

'You encouraged him to race.'

'He's a big boy.'

And even while his head ached, Ken was amused by the tussling between the siblings. This must have been their life – he guessed their father had been a distant one, what with his political career and the business to run. So the kids had probably been raised by nannies and maids, relying on each other more than on their parents. They were quite different in each other's company to how they were with the rest of the world. 'I'll live,' he told them.

'I'll take you to the emergency room,' insisted Oliver.

'I don't need a hospital.'

'Well, you don't need a cabaret show.'

'He should be in one.'

'I don't—'

'We're going.'

Oliver drove them to the Southern California Hospital in Culver City. Coraline arched an eyebrow as her brother helped Ken inside with a hand under his elbow, but said nothing.

'I'm okay. This isn't necessary,' Ken insisted as he gave the attending nurse his details. Only he knew it probably was, but he had no idea how he was going to pay for it.

'Better safe than sorry, pal.'

A doctor came and looked into his eyeballs, took his temperature and blood pressure and seemed, to Ken's wallet, to be running up bills for the sake of it. At the end of it, he was pronounced fit to go, given a pack of aspirin that came out at a buck a pill and went back to reception. 'Where do I pay?' he asked.

The receptionist looked confused. 'You want to pay *again*?' And she looked over to where Oliver stood. Ken understood and thanked her. He didn't thank his friend, because that would only have embarrassed them both. Better to take it as an unspoken part of friendship.

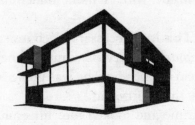

Chapter 7

They got back to the house, Ken easing himself out of the car and trying to keep a lid on the pain in his chest. There was another automobile on the drive and the wisp of a smile spread on Coraline's lips.

'Our grandfather's here,' Oliver explained.

Up the stairs, Ken heard a gravelly English voice spilling from the library. '... come across as cold. Be strong, yes, cultivate that image. But don't be a cold fish,' it said.

Coraline was first through the door, then her brother, and Ken brought up the rear. An aged man with a spark in his eye was revealed. He was in a wheelchair and had a blanket over his knees, but there was something about him that said he could have jumped up and shaken out a foxtrot if he had wanted to. The Governor was behind his desk, listening close.

'Hello, my girl,' the old man said as Coraline kissed him on the cheek.

'Ken Kourian, my grandfather, Simeon Tooke.'

'Pleased to meet you, sir,' Ken said, holding out a hand.

'You too, my boy. Why are you limping?'

'Ken had an argument with a horse.'

'It looks like the horse won. Tincture of *Arnica montana*, son.' He clapped Ken on the arm. 'You can get it at any drugstore. It will do for the swelling and the bruises I observe are just budding out under your shirt.'

'Grandfather was a doctor,' Oliver explained.

'I still am,' the old man admonished. 'Now, children, I need to speak to your father for a while. If he wants to be popular, he has to understand people a bit better than he does.'

'We'll be downstairs.'

They left the two men to it. And as Ken lowered himself down the stairs, he heard the old man's voice again. 'Yes, people vote for a man who gets things done. But they *campaign* for a man they want to spend a day with. You need more warmth to come across. And splash out for other people more. They like that. They stay loyal for that.'

'My father listens to Grandfather more than anyone,' Oliver explained. 'For a retired doctor, he sure knows politics.'

'He seems a good man.'

'He is. He's always been generous. When he came over from England he brought his servants with him. He sent their kids to school. Their grandkids, even.' They reached the ground level. 'Will you stay for supper?'

'I can't. I need to go home and put some ice on these wounds.'

'That's fair. Want to stop by tomorrow?'

Ken tried not to glance at Coraline as he replied. 'I'll be sure to.'

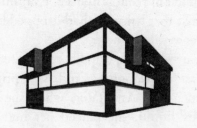

Chapter 8

They spent the next day, Sunday, fishing. Oliver gave Ken a hand from the jetty onto his motor launch. 'Careful, pal. After yesterday you must be broken up.'

'Funny. Real funny.'

'Will you be teasing him all the way, dear brother?' Coraline was sunning herself in a tight red one-piece bathing suit. A wide-brimmed straw hat was keeping her face in the shade.

'Just some of it.'

'That's nice to know.' Ken cursed the accident that had made him a figure for friendly ridicule. Well, maybe she would fall into the sea.

'The pain's pretty much gone, thank you for your

concern,' Ken informed them both. 'Where are the rods?'

He found one and an ice box that contained a cocktail shaker full of ready-mixed cosmopolitan.

'Will you fetch me one of those?' Coraline asked. And he couldn't miss that her voice had dropped half an octave and slowed by a mile an hour.

'Fetch it yourself. I'm a cripple, remember.'

Oliver burst out laughing and Ken poured himself a generous measure. And later, when she had drained away the ruby liquid, she placed her highball glass in front of him and he refilled it without a word and handed it back to her; both of them making sure their fingers didn't touch.

It was the kind of day Ken dreamed about: good friends on the open water, a picture in the can ready to be turned into an actual talkie. When he had taken the long railroad out from Boston, he had pictured scenes like this. They might have been in nightclubs or at the races, but the basic elements – excitement, friendship – were just the same. He glanced at Oliver. Despite the brilliant sun, there seemed to be a shadow across his face.

'You okay?' Ken asked.

Oliver looked blankly at him, as if he had just been woken from a dream. 'Oh, sure. Fine, pal.'

'Something on your mind?'

'On my mind.' Oliver looked at the birds above.

'What is it?'

Oliver took his time to answer. 'You ever think about guilt, Ken?'

That was a heavy question. 'Guilt? As a concept? Sometimes. Not often.' It was the same subject that had weighed on Oliver's mind the night of the boxing match.

'No, no, I guess most people don't.' He rubbed his forehead. 'My father and I ... well, I have a lot to say about guilt.'

'You feel guilty about something?'

'Yes.'

'And you want to talk to your father about it.'

'I do.'

'Have you tried?'

'I've started. The book is just the beginning.'

They were distracted by movement behind them. Coraline stood, reached out her arms and dived neatly under the surface of the water. She came up again a few yards away and turned onto her back, floating in the midday sun.

When Ken looked back to Oliver, the shadow was gone and his friend's face held a warm smile. 'I've bought us all tickets to *Mourning Becomes Electra* tomorrow night,' Oliver said.

'I thought that was sold out.'

'I managed to get hold of some seats.'

Ken guessed they were good ones.

They returned home in the late afternoon. The Governor's political get-together was about to begin and fifteen well-fed men dragged themselves out of black sedans arriving one after another into the driveway. A few of them had to be helped out.

The Governor was in the kitchen, reading over some notes before making his entrance. He looked up when his son and daughter and their friend entered. 'I have a meeting in here in two minutes,' he said.

'Who with?' Coraline asked.

'Burrows.'

'What does he want?'

'I'm not interested in what he wants. I have a task for him.'

'On 402?'

'That's right.'

'It's an absurd bill and it's not even popular. I told you to drop—'

'Sometimes, my girl,' he interrupted her, 'you have to do things that are not popular. You understand politics, Coraline, but you don't understand duty.'

'Duty?'

'*Calling.* I tried to instruct you, but it never sunk in. Bill 402 is my duty and I will not be deterred or derailed by anyone. Not even my own family.'

Coraline paused. 'Do you want us to leave?'

He pondered for a second. 'No, stay. Your presence adds to the atmosphere.'

Ken didn't like being part of the Governor's political scheme, whatever it was, and looked for an exit. Before he found one, a man so fat his vest buttons were strained shuffled into the room.

'Governor,' the obese man said, by way of polite greeting.

'Senator.' The Senator peered at the three young people

in the room. 'I have asked my son and daughter and their friend Mr Kourian to wait here and watch what happens,' Tooke said.

Senator Burrows sniffed nonchalantly. He had an accent from another state. Ken thought it might even be his own Georgia. When he spoke long words, he broke them into single syllables. 'You think, sir, that I'm gonna be in-tim-i-da-ted by a few kids?'

'I'm a busy man. I want to get down to business.'

'Business? Well, sure.' He straightened up, lifting his crown by an inch. 'The President does not want—'

Tooke raised the palm of his hand for silence. 'Do you mean President Roosevelt?'

Burrows seemed confused by the question. 'Of course. He does not want—'

'That man with polio? Crippled by polio?' Burrows was taken aback by the description. 'Did you hear that he fell out of his wheelchair? Right out. There he was, kicking his legs about on the soil like a dying bug.'

Tooke waited for a reply. Eventually, the Senator had to give one. 'The President has a medical condition—'

'No, sir, influenza is a medical condition. Gout is a medical condition. Being crippled with polio is an over-whelming reason he should never have been elected.'

Ken recalled Oliver telling him that, as a boy, polio-myelitis had left him wheelchair-bound. Ken glanced at his friend side-on. There was no reaction to be seen.

'What do you mean by that?' Burrows demanded.

'What do I mean? I mean that a man who cannot get to his feet should not try to lead a nation. A nation that has enemies foreign and domestic. He has my sympathy, like any cripple has. But he should have been barred from office.'

'Your personal feelings about the President's state of health will change nothing. He will not agree to fund this kind of hokey science. It is—'

Tooke interrupted him again, this time by speaking right over Burrows's head to a man standing in the doorway. He was kindly-looking, with very thick spectacles and a bushy moustache that almost hid a hare lip. 'Come in, Doctor. Come on in,' the Governor said, beckoning him into the room. 'Senator, this is Dr Arnold Kruger. He comes to us from the American Eugenics Society. Doctor, the Senator and I were just discussing how much money we can find to aid your work.'

'Governor!' Burrows cried angrily. 'The eugenics movement is gaining ground in Europe right now, but I'm damned if I'll let it take root here.'

Tooke stepped forward and snarled. 'Do not raise your voice in my house. This is where my family live and every brick is ours. You raise your voice and I will have you whipped in the street.' Burrows looked furious but bit his tongue. 'That's better. Now, understand this: the President is a sick man in a sick body. He should never have been allowed to get this far. And I will tell you something. I will have your support for 402.'

Burrows could hold himself no longer. 'And why would I do that?'

'Because if you don't, I will rezone and twist about every electoral district in this state to ensure you never set foot in the Capitol again. You'll be lucky to pull together a thousand votes.'

'I'll put you in jail!'

'I'll take the chance. And do you know why?'

Burrows's fat frame began to shake with anger. 'Why?'

'Because this God-given science will transform our land into a nation. The glory of Rome, sir, was no accident. It was breeding. And now we have a scientific way of ensuring that glory.' Burrows stared at the doctor, whose thick eyebrows beetled behind his thick glasses.

Ken and his friends ate out on the sand below the house that evening, grilling the sandbass they had caught earlier over smoking coals. No table, just cloths laid on the soft ground. The Governor and his father had returned to Sacramento, so it was just them in the house.

As he lay back, his fingers knitted underneath his head, Ken felt happier than he had for some time. LA had been a gamble, for sure, and for the most part a lonely one. But in the warm evening, on the sand, with people around him, he could see a future for himself here in this city.

'What's on your mind, Oliver?' Coraline asked as they tipped their final glasses up around eleven.

'My new book mostly.'

'Worried it won't sell well?'

'Maybe I'm just worried.'

'That's not like you.'

Oliver got to his feet. 'I think I'll go to bed,' he said. 'Ken, why don't you stay in the guest room tonight? Jennings will be here at eight, he can run you home.'

'Thanks.'

'And tomorrow, we can talk about what's been on my mind. All three of us, I think. It concerns you too,' he told Coraline.

'What's going on?' Ken asked.

'I want your opinion. Your advice.'

'About?'

Oliver hesitated. 'It's kinda about the book. But it's wider than that.'

'We can talk now if you want.'

Oliver thought it over. 'No, I'll wait until tomorrow. I want to sleep on it anyhow,' he said. He lifted a hand in farewell and went into the house.

Coraline sipped her vodka martini. A single drop of the misty liquid hung on her lip until her tongue flicked it away. Ken watched out of the corner of his eye.

'It's a hot night,' she said as she lay back.

He nodded. 'It is that.' Of course he wanted to pull her to him. But at that moment, he couldn't see the shot. 'It gets hotter in Georgia. A hundred degrees down there.'

There was a long silence before she broke it.

'I'll bet it does.' And at that, she twisted over and onto her feet. Then she was walking away to the house, following her brother. 'Goodnight,' she said.

'Goodnight.' And when she had crossed the threshold, he also stood and sauntered, hands in pockets, towards his room for the night. Maybe he should have gone for it, shot or no shot.

His room was wide and deep, overlooking the bay. He stripped off his shirt and lay, smoking, for a while – he didn't usually, but they had had a few drinks – wondering what had happened to undermine Oliver's mood.

After a while, he heard a mechanical whine on the wind. Peeling back the curtain, he saw Oliver's launch closing in on the writing tower. A silhouetted figure was piloting the pale boat and another stood behind him. What was going on? Presuming it was Oliver at the wheel, he must have taken some care to leave the house quietly.

Ken returned to his bed and for ten or fifteen minutes he thought more about what had happened that day, how Coraline had looked in her swimsuit. But he kept returning to that sight of two figures in the launch.

There was nothing else for it. He had to investigate. As he left his room, though, he was distracted by a creaking at the other end of the corridor. The blue glass door to Coraline's room was ajar.

He waited. No one came, no one spoke. Was the door open as an oversight? Just for the breeze? Something else? Impossible to say. He walked towards it. The gap between it and its frame was no more than an inch, but air was filtering through from an open window.

Of their own accord, his fingers touched the cool glass, ready to push it open. But a sound stopped them, halted in mid-air. It was a sound unexpected and weighted with threat: a sound like a distant explosion. It echoed once, twice around the bay. Ken couldn't tell what had made it, but after the sight of the boat powering towards the writing tower in the middle of the night, he knew something was wrong.

He rushed back to his room and looked out. The tower was black against a purple sky. He ran to Oliver's door and rapped hard. No answer. He wrenched it open.

Inside, the room was perfectly neat and the bed hadn't been slept in. Ken dashed out, through the marble ballroom, down to the beach and stared out at the stone structure, which looked brutal now against the moonlit skyline. Then he stripped to his underwear and charged into the waves.

They were cold and hard, and higher than they had been during the day. He powered through, crawl-stroke, taking short breaths when the swell lifted him and crashed him down again. Yard by yard, he came closer to the rocky outpost of land. All the way, he burned to know what he would find inside that squat stone tower.

Soon his muscles ached with the effort, but he was too far out to turn back. And then he was grabbing the warm rocks with both hands. The launch wasn't there, he noted.

The room was in pitch blackness when he stepped in and he groped for the oil lamp that had hung from the rafter, but found only empty air. He stumbled against something wooden and his foot connected with an object that rang like metal – the lamp. He lit its flame with a box of matches that he discovered by feeling blindly around on the desk. The lamp hissed into life, throwing yellow light on the room, the books, the furniture; and then upon the lifeless body of Oliver Tooke, sitting behind his writing desk, with his back to the wall and his neck torn to shreds by a bullet. Ken felt all the air leave his lungs.

He had seen a dead body once, but it had been his

grandfather laid out in a coffin, wearing his best suit, and his hands clasped neatly, as if he was trying to look nice on a date. Ken, aged ten, had looked on the peaceful corpse with little more than a child's inquisitiveness.

Now he stared at the form of his friend: the life ripped from it, the blood that had moved it spread on books and flung to the wind. There was a small revolver on the desk, next to the hand that had pulled the trigger to tear a man's throat apart.

'Jesus, Oliver. What have you done?' he asked, wanting an answer. He stood there for a time that could have been a minute, could have been an hour; wanting to know why. Just why.

And there was another who would need to know. Coraline, asleep in her blue-doored bedroom. He had little idea how he would break the news to her. All he could do was turn around and prepare for the cold, aching return to shore. Ken cast a last glance at what had once been a man, and stepped to the threshold.

As he did so, something caught his eye: the secretary cabinet in the corner. It held those dime-books with short-skirted women on one cover and dark-coated men on the other. On top of the pile was *The Turnglass*, Oliver's effort at a similar trick-book. The one he had said earlier in the evening he needed to talk to Ken and Coraline about. He never would now.

Ken still hadn't had a chance to pick up a copy, as filming and work had crowded out his daily life. Now he opened it and read again the first line. 'Simeon Lee's grey eyes were visible . . .' He turned it over. As Oliver had said, his story had been paired with another writer's, some run-of-the-mill spook tale titled *The Waterfall*.

Why would Oliver need Ken's advice about the book? And why hadn't he asked for it then and there? There was a chance that it was important; that the novel would give a clue to Oliver's state of mind of late. But that would have to wait: Coraline was in the house and he had to return with the painful news. Without the motor boat, he would have to swim back, and he could hardly carry the book. He would have to leave it here.

He prepared for the exertion. His body remembered the cold and the drag of the current, and tensed like stone before he dived.

It took all his energy reserves to crawl and kick back to the shore, finally pulling himself onto the sand and breathing heavily. At the edge of his vision, a few hundred yards along the bay, he saw what he was sure was the launch, beached. The current might have brought it over.

Or someone had powered it to shore and abandoned it.

He pulled on his pants and hurried through the ballroom and the entrance hall, up the white marble stairs and along to Coraline's room. All the way, he knew that this had become a different house to the one where he had spent happy days.

Her door was open still, wafting in the breeze, as if the room itself was breathing. His hand pushed it open.

'Hello, Ken,' she said softly, as soon as he entered, as if she had been waiting for him. And he saw, in the blue moonlight, Coraline turn over in bed to face him. She was wearing something made of silk decorated with aquamarine stars. He didn't reply but took a step forward. 'No words? No invitation. Just walking in?' Her lips caught a flash of the light. 'Ken?'

'Coraline. I'm sorry.'

'Sorry about what?'

'Something's happened.' He sat on the corner of the bed. He could make out her expression now: quizzical, amused. She waited for him to continue and he searched for the words that would soften the blow he was about to deal her. He hated that it was happening here, now, with the two of them like this. But in the end he could only be direct. 'Oliver has shot himself.'

Even as he said it, he had his doubts that that was the truth; but this wasn't the time.

She flinched as if he had hit her. Then she sat bolt upright. '*What?* What do you mean?'

'He's dead. I'm sorry. I found him in the writing tower.'

She flung back the covers. She breathed deeply twice, down into her core, and pulled on an emerald-coloured satin kimono that hung over the back of a chair. She spoke calmly. 'You've been tricked. He's not dead. It's some sort of a trick.'

A trick. No, no, if only that were true.

'I'm sorry, but I saw him.'

'There's no reason for him to do that!' she hissed. She strode to the drapes and threw them open. The moon – a pale sickle – was dead ahead, dropping milky light onto the stone tower in the sea. She pointed. 'Is he still there?' she asked.

'Yes.' So she had, at least, accepted it.

'I want him back here. I want you to bring him back.'

'I can't.'

'Why not?'

'We need to call the authorities. An ambulance.'

'And what good would that do now?' she demanded icily.

'It's what we need to do.'

She turned to him. Her eyes bore into his. 'Oliver would never do this.'

He could feel the salt on his body, smell the sweat in the air. 'I'll call the police. They need to be notified.'

She watched him leave.

It took twenty minutes for an unmarked police car to arrive at the house. 'Detective Jakes,' a gruff officer said by way of introduction. He was in his fifties, body gone to seed, and sported a moustache that he scratched with his pencil as if colouring in bald spots. 'He's where?' he asked with surprise when the location of the body was explained to him. Ken, now dressed, took him to the beach and pointed. 'Jesus above. How the hell you even get there?'

'The motorboat.' Ken pointed to it.

Jakes swore again. 'All right. Police ambulance is on its way. You know how to run that thing?'

'Sure. But . . .'

'But what?'

Something made Ken look up at the house. The dark figure of Coraline was staring down, with a cigarette glowing red between her fingers. She pulled the drapes across and was gone.

'I'll tell you later.'

'Whatever you say. Let's get going.'

They got going. And soon they were cutting through the waves, then scrambling onto the rocks that had become a tomb for Oliver Tooke's body. Ken let the detective go first. The oil lamp was still burning and the room was as he had left it: threatening and bloody.

Jakes scrutinized the scene, then looked back and raised his eyebrows.

'Yeah, I know,' Ken muttered.

'He do or say anythin' to suggest he was gonna do this?'

'Nothing.'

'Well,' Jakes shrugged. 'Truth is, not many do. With most, it's "He seemed a bit down, but not so bad he was gonna kill himself."' He paused. 'I'm sorry for your loss.'

The phrase was empty. Ken didn't believe Detective Jakes was any bit sorry for his loss. It was form, though, like taking your hat off indoors.

'So what do we do now?'

'Well, there's nothin' suspicious far as I can see. Weapon right there under his hand. Now we just take him back to land. I'm sorry for your loss.'

'Yeah, you said.' He didn't care that he sounded rude.

'We can wait for the ambulance to turn up and come over the same way we did. But be honest with you, it's not gonna be any more dignified than if we just take him back ourselves. Your choice, though.'

Given that choice, it seemed more respectful to take Oliver back themselves instead of watching him carried by strangers who had probably taken five other corpses that week. That day, even; this was LA, after all.

And so they lifted him between them into the small boat and headed back to the headland. But before they did that, as Jakes's back was turned, Ken picked up Oliver Tooke's final story, *The Turnglass*, and slipped it inside his jacket. Little doubts were crawling into his mind like ants, so he wanted to know what the book held – and he wasn't sure the policeman would understand.

Once ashore, they laid the dead man in his bed, with a sheet up to his chin to hide the violence that the bullet had wreaked. As if it mattered now.

Coraline was sitting in an armchair in the corner of her room when he got there. 'Would you like to see Oliver?' he asked.

Without a word, she walked to her brother's bedroom, gazed at the body and returned to her own room.

'Detective,' Ken began, as they went down to the kitchen. It was time to let loose what he had seen earlier.

Jakes was writing something in his notebook. 'Yeah?' He didn't look up.

'I think I saw two people going out there.'

'What d'you mean?' He was still concentrating on his notes.

'In the boat. When I saw the boat going out, I think there were two people in it.'

He paused. 'You think? I mean, you sure?'

Ken closed his eyes and dragged the image out, as plain as day. 'I'm sure. I saw two people.'

Jakes tapped his pencil on his notepad thoughtfully. 'How? You got night-time sun out here?'

'There was enough moonlight.'

Jakes looked like he had chewed something sour and went back to writing. 'Moonlight nothin'.'

Ken tried another tack. 'He bought us all tickets to a play tomorrow night. Is that what a man who's planning on ending his own life would do?'

'I ain't a shrink.'

'But if—'

'Listen.' Jakes closed his notebook. 'You seem to be suggestin' there's foul play here. Well, I hear ya, but there's nothin' at all about this that says so. You said yourself Mr Tooke seemed unhappy yesterday evening, he went out to this crazy outhouse he has on a bunch of rocks – I have no idea how that's legal, by the way – and he uses his own gun.'

'How do you know it's his?'

'What? The rod?'

'Yes.'

'No reason to think it ain't.'

'That's not good enough.'

'And the angle of the bullet.' He demonstrated with his pencil. 'It comes up through the neck an' out the side. If someone else shot it, he woulda had to be sittin' in the victim's lap.'

'You can't be sure of that.'

'Okay, okay.' He put the notebook and pencil into his inside breast pocket. 'Let's say my opinion about this event is based on twenty-five years as a detective. Because in all that time, I have never seen a fake gun planted or a suicide that was anything except what it looked to be: an unhappy man with the means to end things. And I'm sorry. I really am. But we can't help the facts.'

'Can you check it for fingerprints?'

The detective was quiet for a moment. 'Look, Mr Kourian. We can do that. We can try to trace it right back to the manufacturer. We could knock on every door from here to Tijuana askin' people if they've seen anythin'. But I'm gonna level with you: we won't. Because there is absolutely nothin' about this raises any suspicions.'

The doorbell rang and Ken went out to find the police ambulance. The driver apologized for the time it had taken and explained that they had had to stop at every house on the road to ask for directions because he had no idea where in God's name he was. And then the body was taken away, and Jakes drove off and it was just Ken and Coraline alone in Turnglass House. He found her in her room, back in bed in her silk nightdress with aquamarine stars.

'They've all gone,' he said.

'I know.'

'Do you want me to telephone your father?'

'Don't you think it should come from someone he's met more than twice?' Her rejection was offhand, but given the circumstances he couldn't fault her.

'I'll go back to my apartment and leave you in peace,' he said.

He collected his few things – his billfold, his keys – and called for a taxi to take him back to town. As he ducked down into the car, he thought for a moment that the cab had a radio drawling out piano music and he was about to ask the driver to turn it off; but then he realized the music was coming from within the house. Coraline was playing the white baby grand in the ballroom. Something European and melancholy.

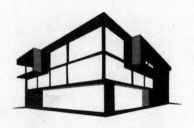

Chapter 9

He crawled into his bed around six, and lay there staring at the ceiling, from time to time hearing the couple in the next room argue. They were awake earlier than usual too. It was the heat, no doubt, that had forced them out of their sultry bed.

The detective, Jakes, was convinced it was suicide. Ken hated that because the thought that his only real friend had cut his life short tasted as bitter as brine. But he needed to look at it objectively, so he tried to think of a reason why Oliver might have done it. He had no money worries, for sure; his work was in demand; and if he was in debt, say, he could have tapped his father for cash.

A love affair that ditched? There had been no sign at all

that Oliver had been secretly involved with someone. He hadn't even seemed all that interested in girls – or men, for that matter.

And all that was without the image in Ken's brain of two men going out on that launch. Sure, it was dark, but he had seen what he had seen. So the questions were: who was the second man, and what were they doing out there?

Well, there was one item Ken had lifted from the scene that might help. Oliver had said he had something on his mind, something he needed to talk to Ken and Coraline about, and it was connected to his new book.

The Turnglass turned out to be a hypnotic story about an English doctor investigating the deaths of his relatives during the previous century in the county of Essex – where Oliver had said his family were from. The action took place in a strange house on the coast that could be cut off from the mainland by the tide – and it had the same name as the family's place in California: Turnglass House. So that had to be the Tookes' ancestral home. Yet another connection was that the doctor was named after Oliver's grandfather, Simeon; one of the characters even had Oliver's own name. There was cruelty in the tale, Ken found. Flicking through the pages, a woman's suffering stood out.

I checked the clock in the corner. 'Nearly an hour. She cannot last for much longer. The chill must be into her bones.' I shut the book and removed my spectacles, so I could better concentrate. The sound of her wailing rose again. It had been angry, then plaintive and was now outwardly threatening.

It was odd, but there was even a story within the story, a bleak novelette named *The Gold Field* about a California family living in a house made entirely of glass. That tale's narrator was searching for the truth about his mother's death, but only a few brief fragments of the story appeared. They described a sea voyage across the Atlantic, the unnamed narrator's self-doubt and, finally, retribution for a terrible crime.

Ken began to read from the start, but all the time he was searching for a meaning beneath the meaning. He had gotten about a third of the way through without finding a knot in the yarn when his alarm clock rang like hell. It was eight o'clock and time to get up for work at the newspaper. He was in no mood for it – well, he could barely stand – but given the amount of time he had taken off to appear as a bit-player in the movies, his job was already hanging by a thread. The book went into his bedside table.

So, by nine-thirty – late, but not dangerously late – he was in his wooden seat in the *Times* advertising sales office, his mind spinning. It occurred to him that there were a couple of strange or downright suspicious aspects to Oliver's life that should be looked into if Ken wanted to get to the bottom of what had happened to him: one was the unknown reason Oliver had posted bail for Piers Bellen, and Ken would have to track that barking dog down; the other was the Tookes' first family tragedy. He went to the phone and asked the internal operator to connect him to the library department: the keepers of past editions of the paper and files on every subject that came into the news.

'Library.'

'Hello. This is Ken Kourian. I'd like to see the reports from an abduction case in 1915.' He gave the names of Governor Oliver Tooke and his children.

'Okay. It'll take us a couple of hours. Which desk're you on?'

He knew this could bring down the stop sign. 'I'm on classified.'

'Where?'

'Classified advertisements.'

There was a pause. 'Then what the hell d'you want clippings for?'

He had prepared a story. 'A potential advertiser is publishing a book about old crimes in the state. I said we'd help out. It's a juicy contract.' It was a bad story.

Another pause. 'Okay,' the voice conceded with a clear tone of irritation. 'Couple a' hours.'

'Thanks,' he said. 'And one more thing.'

'What now?'

'Can you see if there's anything about Oliver Tooke, the writer, in the files too?'

'When?'

Ken wasn't certain. 'Any time.'

The voice on the other end of the line didn't sound happy. 'You want me to check every edition ever?'

'How about the last twelve months?'

'Okay, okay.'

Four hours later, a copy boy placed a card box on his desk. It contained editions of the *LA Times* from 1915 detailing the crime; the first was from 2 November.

A police manhunt is underway after the infant son of glass magnate Oliver Tooke was kidnapped from the family's ancestral mansion in England.

The boy, Alexander, four, was wrenched from the arms of his mother, Florence, by two gypsy men. Mrs Tooke was walking in the garden with her elder son, Oliver, five, when they set upon her. The English police speculate that the men may have had accomplices. The family is awaiting a ransom demand or other such communication from the criminals.

The family had been spending the summer at the pile in the county of Essex with Mr Tooke's father, Simeon, who immigrated to California in 1883.

Inspector Marlon Long of the Essex County police department said his men would not rest until the boy was back with his family.

Florence. That name made him sit up. He hadn't known it was her name, and there was a woman in Oliver's story named after her. That had to mean something.

Next, the edition from two days later.

Police in the terrible Alexander Tooke kidnapping case have been rousting gypsy camps around Essex, England, searching for the missing infant. More than fifty men have been brought in for questioning, and although three have been charged with unrelated offences, a police source said the

English coppers are none the wiser regarding the whereabouts of the boy. His father, Oliver Tooke, founder of the glass manufacturing firm, has put up a $10,000 reward for information that leads to the safe recovery of the boy.

It was accompanied by a photograph of a family portrait. Ken had seen the picture before: it was the one hanging in the library at Turnglass House. Here, in rough newsprint, it was captioned: 'Mr Tooke with his wife, Florence, and their children, Oliver junior, five, Alexander, four, and Coraline, one.'

There were other reports in the file, but they were just speculation or updates that said nothing – until a story a year later.

The tragic Tooke family have left England to return to their home on Point Dume, Los Angeles. Ever since the kidnapping of little Alex, four, the family have been holed up in their ancestral home on a small island in the county of Essex, on the eastern coast of Great Britain, with the shutters closed. Oliver Tooke offered greater and greater sums of money for information about the whereabouts of the boy, with the reward now standing at a huge $30,000. But to no avail. Their return indicates that they have now given up hope of seeing the poor little boy alive again.

And there was one final, harsh clipping. A report from 1920 splashed right across the page, headlined: 'Family curse strikes Tookes once more as mother drowns'.

> Florence Tooke, wife of glass magnate Oliver Tooke, has drowned while the family were on vacation in England, visiting their ancestral seat on the island of Ray in the coastal county of Essex. To outsiders, the family seem cursed, having suffered the abduction and presumed murder of their younger son, Alexander, at the same location some five years ago. Mrs Tooke was reported to have been walking across a mud bank when the cruel tide rose and submerged her. Her husband is said by friends to be 'totally distraught' and is doing his best to comfort the couple's remaining children, Oliver junior, ten, and Coraline, six.

The story continued underneath a bleary picture of a slight woman dressed for an evening of dancing, with dark hair loose about her shoulders.

> Mrs Tooke was a society beauty. Born Florence De Waal in New York, she was reputed to be a fine watercolourist in the impressionist style and hosted artistic salons, settling down as a patroness of the arts after her marriage. In recent years, she organized exhibitions of works by artists on the Western Front. Some were controversial, prompting accusations of defeatism and moral turpitude.

At the bottom of the box was the sole recent story about the younger Oliver Tooke. It was from the social pages and an anonymous writer was linking the 'hot young pen-man' to two or three 'sizzling starlets' at some party or other.

> But friends, don't think Olly Tooke's life is a bed of roses. You may remember the Tooke kidnapping case twenty years ago – his brother abducted and never found. His mother dead a few years after that from a broken heart, having pined away for her lost boy. So is Olly hot because he can turn a sharp phrase, or is it his family notoriety and sun-kissed looks? Will his star keep shooting or will he be kicked out of the night sky? Only time will tell. But you know where to come to find out!

Jesus Christ, that was exploitative stuff, Ken thought to himself. *Give the man a break.*

He was drumming his fingers on the desk thoughtfully when his boss returned. 'Hey, George. I'm not feeling well,' he said.

'What's the matter?'

'Something I ate. I need to go home, I think.'

'If you're cutting out early to go to one of your screen tests ...'

'I'm not. I'm sick.'

George jerked his thumb at the way out. 'Okay, just come in early tomorrow if you can to make up.'

'Okay.'

Ken pulled on his jacket just as the telephone trilled and

George picked it up. 'Classifieds.' There was a pause, then George held it out. 'For you.'

Ken took it. 'Hello?'

'Hello, Ken.'

He knew the voice. Very few women called him – one or two secretaries and that was it. This voice was thirty years younger than them. 'Coraline.'

There was a slight hesitation. 'Can you meet me?'

For some reason, he wasn't sure how to answer. Then form took over. She was, after all, a bereaved sister. 'Of course. Where?'

George looked up, his brow furrowing as if he had just heard something he didn't understand but didn't like. Ken pretended he hadn't seen.

'There's a bar on Rodeo Drive called the Yacht Club. Half an hour.'

'I can make that. See you there.'

She hung up and he did the same.

'Feeling better?' George asked sarcastically.

'Her brother died last night,' he replied. He caught sight of the file of cuttings on his desk. He hoped George wouldn't spot it, or it might start to look strange.

'Okay, okay, go. But in future, don't tell me you're sick when you're not. I'm not an ogre. We need to look after each other.'

'Sure.' He went out feeling a little guilty.

Chapter 10

The bar turned out to be an upmarket place full of movie types. A few want-to-be-actresses sat individually at the bar nursing overpriced drinks and hoping to be spotted.

Coraline wore a tight black dress and pillbox hat with a silk ribbon twisted around it. 'Thank you for coming,' she said formally.

'Not at all.' He felt an urge to make it less formal, but held himself back and signalled to a waiter. 'What's happened this morning?'

'I went to the morgue to formally identify him. My father will arrange the funeral.' She drank from a highball of mint julep.

'Burial?'

The word made her flinch ever so slightly. 'We have a family plot. Oliver wasn't religious – neither am I – so it hardly seems to matter where or how, really.' Was that true? Even those who didn't bother God any more than He bothered them cared where they were laid to rest. She paused. 'He talked about guilt a lot recently.'

'He talked about it to me too. What does it mean?'

'Something on his conscience. I don't know.' She drained her glass and ordered another.

Ken just came out with it, loaded as the words were. 'So, you think he did it himself?'

She fixed him with milky blue eyes and tapped a cigarette out of a packet of Nat Shermans. 'Do you have a reason for thinking otherwise?' Her voice didn't falter.

He had a few splinters here and there that wouldn't have made a safety match. 'A couple of things,' he said. 'He didn't seem depressed; not to me anyway. Did you know he had a gun?'

'No, I didn't.'

It was the sort of thing you would know about your brother. But he stored that thought for now. 'So it might not even be his.'

She drank half the golden-brown julep without flinching. 'Possibly not.'

'And I saw two men go out in that boat.'

She paused lifting her cigarette to her lips. He studied her reaction, trying to pin it down. 'To his writing tower?'

'That's right.'

'Are you certain?'

'I am. But I have to tell you that Detective Jakes isn't convinced. He thinks it was too dark to see.'

'And what's your response to that?'

'That there was a moon and light enough.'

She wrapped her lips around the cigarette and blew a line of smoke to her side. 'That's not exactly conclusive,' she replied.

'No, it isn't.'

'So do I take it on trust that you saw what you think you saw?'

'I guess you have to.' He watched her lift her drink again. 'I pulled the stories that the *Times* ran about your brother Alexander. His abduction.'

With a flash of bitterness, she placed her drink hard down on the zinc table. 'Well, aren't you the little sleuth?' She composed herself again. 'That was a long time ago.'

'Do you—'

'I was a year old. So no, I don't remember a thing.' The air was heavy between them.

'I went to a party at the house a few months back. A man called Piers Bellen gave me a ride home – or he was meant to. He attacked a coloured man at a diner on the way and we ended up in the police station instead. Oliver bailed him out.' She listened without reaction. 'But the really screwy thing is that when Bellen called him, he said Oliver had better come down there and post bail or ... he said something

99

queer as hell about Oliver never knowing what Piers had found out.'

She thoughtfully tapped ash into a glass tray. 'We should speak to him.'

'Agreed.'

First, they would have to find him, though, because Ken had no way to contact Bellen.

But there was someone who did.

'You fucking abandoned me to that pig!' Gloria yelled down the telephone line. Ken and Coraline were in the lobby call booth and it was a wonder the earpiece didn't shatter. He hadn't spoken to Gloria since the neuralgia-inducing night at the police station.

'You wanted to go with him.'

'No, I didn't! I saw him twice. No, three times after that. That's all. I thought he was a big-time producer.'

'So what is he really?'

'What is he? He works for the fucking government,' she sneered. 'State Department, I think. You want to speak to him, call him there.' She hung up.

The State Department. Foreign affairs. Something to do with the family's time in England, maybe. The disappearance of Oliver's brother. Maybe.

After going through information and two DC switchboards, Ken got through to Bellen.

'Ken who?' he huffed. 'Oh, from the party. Did you see what that shine did to me, I—' he spluttered.

'Did you hear about Oliver?' Ken interrupted.

'Tooke? Hear what about that ass?'

'He's dead.'

A pause. 'Wh ... how?' And did Bellen sound fearful, instead of shocked? Yeah, maybe.

'He died in that stone building he has off the shore; the one he goes to to write. Gunshot.'

'Jesus Chr—' He sounded like he had just seen a man coming towards him with a blackjack in one hand and a noose in the other.

But Ken wasn't in the mood to molly-coddle. 'Tell me, Piers.'

Another pause. And then drawled suspicion. 'Tell you what?'

'Tell me what you had over him.'

Hesitation. 'Nothing.'

'Was it about Alexander?'

'*Alexander?*' He snorted in derision. 'No, it wasn't about *Alexander*.' There was much in the way he said it. But his arrogance was also his undoing, because it told Ken where to go next.

'So it was about someone else. Someone else close to him.' And as he spoke, Ken's hand went, unconsciously, to the book in his jacket pocket and flicked the edges of the pages. There was something in there that he had been thinking about a lot. It was the way one of the characters had been given the name of Oliver's dead mother. And on the phone to Oliver, Bellen had caricatured a frightened woman's voice. 'It was about Florence, wasn't it?' Silence. Guilty silence, for sure. Ken's arrow might have been shot half-blind, but it had gone right through its mark. 'What was it about her that you were holding over him?'

His voice became angry. 'You asshole, I—'

'You had something over him about Florence Tooke. And I'm guessing you got it through your work. So you tell me what it was, or I inform your superiors that you've been doing a little freelancing in office hours.'

There was a long hiss on the line. 'He wanted to know about . . . how she died. How exactly.'

He saw Coraline stiffen a little.

'She drowned herself,' Ken said. The newspaper reports had been clear as day.

'But that's just it,' Bellen replied. Ken could feel something coming through the bar, a freight train with failed brakes. 'They held a coroner's inquest. I had a copy of the report sent over. I passed it on to Tooke.'

'What did it say?' Ken prompted him.

'It was the jury . . .' He trailed off.

'What about them?'

'They . . .' He hesitated again, as if the fear of what could come of spilling the facts was rearing in his mind.

'Talk.'

'They . . . returned an open verdict.'

A what? 'What the hell does an open verdict mean?'

'It means they were suspicious. A witness – the house-keeper or something – said Mrs Tooke was pretty happy that day. Took her painting set out to make some art. Didn't seem like she was going to do herself in.' Ken glanced at Coraline; he hoped the words wouldn't be too hard on her. 'So the jury thought it could've been an accident; could've been suicide. Could've been . . . something else. That's what it means.'

Could've been ... something else. It sank in. Coraline's only reaction as she listened was to bow her forehead a little. It was about as emotional as Ken had seen her get, and that wasn't saying much.

'What else do you know?' Ken asked.

'Nothing. Zilch. It took me a long time to get that. And I wanted to—'

Ken hung up. It was obvious that what Bellen had wanted was to milk Oliver for all he could.

For the best part of a minute, Coraline stared across the room at the movie men with girls half their age. Then she spoke. 'Some time ago, Oliver disappeared for a while – a month, I guess.'

'You think he was over in England?'

'When he came back, he was ... distant.'

'There was something he found there.'

'I should say so.'

She put the check on her account and they left the club. Ken followed her to an empty lot where a building would probably go up within a year. For now, it was a scrub of grass and hobos. Ken gave her some space. 'What do you think, Ken?' she asked without looking at him.

'Your father never said anything about doubts over her death?'

'Of course not.'

'Then I think there's a lot we need to know,' he replied. 'And we won't find it by standing here.'

She understood. 'You think we need to go to England?'

'Yeah, I do.'

She reached into her pocket book, took out a fresh Nat

Sherman and lit it with an electric lighter. She blew three long drags into the air before speaking again. 'I haven't been there for a long time.' She paused. 'I hate that house.'

'Tell me about it.'

'What do you want to know?'

'Start at the beginning.'

'My grandfather inherited it from some distant relative. He—'

'Wait, that's true?'

'What do you mean?'

It seemed as crazy as everything else right then. 'In Oliver's book, there's an English doctor named Simeon who inherits his uncle's house.'

'Is there? I haven't read it. Oliver asked me not to for now, but wouldn't tell me why. He said he'd tell me when I could.'

That itself was strange, very strange.

'Tell me about what happened at Turnglass House. The one in England,' Ken said. 'Was there really a body buried in the mud?'

She looked at him curiously. It must have seemed screwed up to her that there was an outsider who knew some of her family secrets. 'Yes, there was. My grandfather told us that when we were old enough to understand.'

'Then it's the story. It's the story in *The Turnglass*. Though Oliver changes your grandfather's surname.'

She laughed sardonically at the revelation. 'Our great family legend. More than a legend, though, it's true, I'm sure. I think my father is a little proud to be descended from that stock – all the great families have a little murder and madness in them, like mediaeval Popes. All starting with my grandfather – after he inherited the house, he lived there for a while before he came here.'

'Was there a woman imprisoned at the house named Florence? In the story, she's sister-in-law to Simeon's uncle.'

'There was a woman, yes. But she didn't have my mother's name. That's Oliver's choice.'

He nodded thoughtfully. What was Oliver saying by naming the woman after their mother? 'I've started the book. I need to finish it. I think you should too.'

'I'll do it on the way to England.'

'All right. There's just one hitch.' A hitch was a polite way of saying he had the spending power of a monk.

She didn't have to be telepathic – his worn shoes spoke for him. 'Don't worry, the family fortune will cover it.'

'I'm ...'

'Don't mention it.'

Okay. He turned to the practicalities of travel. 'We have two options.'

'Go on.'

'It'll take a week by boat. Two days if we fly.'

The newsreels had been full of the first transatlantic passenger flights, flitting from New York to Newfoundland to refuel, then to Ireland for yet more gas and finally coming in to the port of Southampton on the southern English coast. The flights were in huge sea planes that took off from coastal harbours rather than inland aerodromes.

'Then we fly.'

'If we can get seats.'

'My father is the Governor of California. We'll get seats.'

'Even if it's full?'

'They'll make it less full.'

'I guess they will.' So they were going to England, where her brother had disappeared and her mother drowned. Everything had to be connected to one – or both – of those events. He put his hands in his pockets. This open street with men and women on their ways to grocery shops and streetcar stops wasn't the place for what he was about to ask, but he had little choice. 'What do you remember about your mother's death?'

She stared at the cigarette between her fingers and threw it aside. 'I was in the library, reading. Something about English kings and queens.' Ken could barely think of her as a girl instead of the fashionable young woman in front of him. 'Father came in. He was walking very slowly, I remember that. And he told me straight up that Mother was gone. She had gone out onto the mudflats. We never recovered her body.' Ken gave her a moment to breathe. 'Every year, we went back on the anniversary. Stayed for a week. I stopped when I turned twenty-one, but Father still visits. It's right about now. I always loathed going – as if she would care that we were there.'

It took thirty-six hours to arrange the flights. In the spare day they didn't see each other, but Ken had arrangements to make: he took two weeks' unpaid vacation from the newspaper. And he had to get through the rest of Oliver's story.

It was a ghost story in some ways. No spooks, but the spirits of the past coming back to haunt the guilty living. They, the spirits, were everywhere, even in music.

She touched her fingers to her heart and began to sing that hymn again. *'Help of the helpless, oh, abide with me.'* And he realized why she sang it over and over: he could just make out the tune itself on the wind. It had to be coming from the bells of the church on Mersea.

Ken followed the characters across their bleak island and through London's winding streets. Through risk and reversal. Friendship and enmity. And when he finally reached the end, he grasped the whole sadness of the story: nobody won. Nobody. No one gained when the buried truth was dug up; or celebrated when the guilty secret was told. Even the characters left standing in the final paragraphs had lost. Reveal the past, it said, and you destroy the present.

That made Ken pause. If Oliver had uncovered secrets and come to wish he hadn't, who was to say that what he found out shouldn't be left to disappear again? But the dog of vengefulness was biting. Look at it hot or cold: Oliver, his friend, was dead and Ken wanted to know who was to pay for it.

The journey began with a regular flight to New York City and then on by railroad to Long Island to pick up the transatlantic airplane at Port Washington.

They had to change trains at Flushing Main Street. The

GARETH RUBIN

platform that morning was crowded with day-trippers and men shifting crates of apples and flour to local stores. Some trains were stopping to pick up a hundred or so passengers, but most were expresses passing straight through at full speed.

Ken's mind had jumped about all morning and had now turned to the relationship between Coraline and her father. He couldn't get a handle on it. She advised her dad on drumming up cash from political supporters, but she sure didn't seem warm towards him. But then she didn't seem warm towards anyone, except maybe Oliver. 'Know anyone who's flown across the Atlantic?' he asked just to make conversation.

'Amelia Earhart.'

'You knew her personally?'

'A little.'

Well, that was cute.

They were swamped by other bodies crowding in, desperate to get onto the next train that called at the station. There was another express coming straight through. Luckily, they had been early on the platform so they would at least have seats when one stopped. Coraline checked her wristwatch. 'Two minutes,' she said.

'Good, I . . .' But at that moment, Ken felt something – someone – stamping hard into the back of his knee, collapsing it; and a shoulder barging him forwards, toppling him over. His feet were leaving the concrete platform and his body was rolling in the air. It was a sickening, tumbling fall. But it was the sight of the rails and blackened stones rising up to meet him that made his heart stop.

Even as he fell, he could see the train, no more than twenty yards away, speeding towards him. There was no time to turn over or grab for the platform. He could only put his hands out to shield his face from the impact. Then it came: smacking down on metal and grit, his head cannoning against the bones of his fingers and his stomach thudding onto the steel rail.

The blow stunned him for a second, but he had no time for that. The sight of the charging train bearing down on him shocked his brain into self-preservation and he rolled to his side, right up against the tawny bricks that formed the platform. Someone screamed. The train siren blared. He felt the heat from the wheels rushing towards him and heard the panicked yells of the people on the platform as they watched a man about to die. But the survival instinct is strong, and Ken pressed himself with every ounce of strength he had into the bricks, as if he could turn his flesh to liquid to crawl into the tiny gaps. And he felt something flicker past the back of his head. Something hard and hot.

He knew then that if he had been a hair's breadth further back, a thousand tons of steel would have smashed his skull to pieces.

Then it was right past him, its wheels screeching, brakes jamming the locomotive into the rails like it would tear them apart. And someone, a woman, was still screaming.

'Is he dead?' 'The train hit him!' 'Did you see?' came yells from among the passengers on the platform. 'Someone pull him up!' Ken risked the slightest movement, a twitch of his head that showed him the train stationary just past him. And he collapsed onto his back on the rough ground.

'There's another one in two minutes!'

Okay, okay. He had no time to rest there. He got that.

Ken curled up into a sitting position and carefully stood, which took him face to face with Coraline, whose pale features seemed even paler now, all the blood having drained from them.

He didn't have time for the cries of 'Are you okay?' that were pouring at him. Now that he was alive, he only wanted to know who had knocked him down. 'Call the cops,' he growled, clambering onto the platform. He was more than ready for a fight. He was spoiling for it.

He stared around, his bloody fists tight, searching for a face coloured with guilt. There were young mothers, old men, children. All looked shocked. None ashamed or disappointed that Ken was still alive and ready to kick like a hard-done-by mule. But through the middle, for a split second and no more, he saw a man standing away from the others, in the mouth of the exit. He was completely ordinary in appearance – average height and build, hair the colour of mud. But there was a look on his face that was knife-edge determination. Then the crowd shifted again and he disappeared. 'Get out the way!' Ken shouted, pushing through, shoving out of his path the people who tried to stop him, telling him he was concussed or needed to take time to breathe. He reached the exit at speed and stared up and down the wide new road outside, but there was no one in sight apart from a couple of mothers with babies in strollers.

A policeman ran into the scene, his face redder than a cherry. Someone must have yelled for him.

'You okay, sport?' the officer asked, his heavy breath rattling in a flabby and unfit body.

'I'm alive.' Ken wiped his brow.

'Real dangerous, this place, when all these folks are shoving,' the cop said, taking off his sweaty cap. He should have wrung it out. 'I've told them about it.'

'Someone pushed me. Deliberately,' Ken said in a dangerous voice.

The cop looked taken aback, as if Ken had accused him of being the kingpin behind the attack. 'No, no, not here. Just an accident. People are always pushing and shoving. Don't often go over, but—'

They were interrupted by the driver of the train, who had climbed out of his cab and run across. 'You okay, sir?' he said. He was just a kid. 'I hit the brakes as soon as I saw. Only they—'

'It's not your fault.'

'Just an accident,' the cop said in a reassuring voice.

'That's the last thing it was,' Ken told him. 'Is there anyone here you recognize?' He pointed to the crowd, who were whispering to each other as they watched the discussion.

'Recognize? A few, I guess.' His tone had soured from defensive to evasive. 'This is my beat. I see the same people all the time.' Ken gave it up. Like he said, he was alive, and what was this flatfoot going to tell him anyhow? Only that the folks round here wouldn't hurt a fly if it settled on their nose. And from now on, Ken would be alive and careful. 'You want to come to the station house, make a statement?' asked the cop. It was obvious that he didn't want Ken to do any such thing. It would cause all sorts of paperwork headaches.

Ken shook his head and led Coraline away into the station, where a coffee cart was sitting with no customers, all of them having squeezed onto the platform to see the spectacle. Cheaper than the talkies. Even the girl who attended the cart had left her post to crane her neck, not realizing that the star of the show was right there behind her. Ken poured two drinks and threw a few coins into the box. He had no idea if they would cover the cost, but he wasn't in much of a mood to check the price list.

'You know that was no accident, right?'

'I know,' Coraline replied. 'What do you think we should do?'

'Given the choice, I'm all for staying alive.' He sipped his coffee; it was awful, but he didn't care. The girl who should have been selling it had returned but was keeping a respectful distance just in case falling in front of a train was a communicable disease. 'Any idea who it was?'

'No,' Coraline said.

'Did you see anyone?'

'No. Did you?'

'I just felt someone knock my legs away. But when I got back up, I saw ...'

'What did you see?'

'Someone. A guy.'

'Did you recognize him?'

'No, but there was something about him, about the way he was looking at me.'

'What does that mean?'

'It was like he planned to do better next time.'

On the harbourside at noon, they stood before a plane the size of a house bobbing in the water.

'That, ma'am,' said an attendant, proud as punch of his charge, 'is a Boeing B-314 Yankee Clipper. Biggest airplane in the world. Ever.'

'It's very impressive,' Coraline said. 'Would you be so kind as to show us to our seats?'

'Glad to, ma'am.'

Coraline thanked him and they were shown into the cabin. It was as luxurious as anything Cunard could sport, with two decks of sink-into-them couches, well-stocked bars and valets in white jackets. The chefs had been hijacked from the best hotels in Washington DC with the promise of a clientele of crowned heads and tips to match them. The nineteen-hour overnight journey would be a vacation in itself.

The plane had seven compartments on the passenger deck, each one holding ten seats, which would be converted into sleeping berths with curtained bunks, all made of polished walnut.

'Quite something, isn't she?' Ken suggested.

'I guess so.'

'Though I wonder how long she'll be flying this route.'

'What do you mean?'

'Your brother and I talked a few times about Germany

and their new Chancellor. Oliver thought war was back on the cards.'

'You thought different?' she replied.

'I did then. Now I'm not so sure. I think Poland's next. I wouldn't be surprised if we're back in. What do you think?'

She thought briefly. 'My father was a lieutenant in the last war. He lost half his men in a single day – and he remembers every one of their names. If he's President, I think we would stay out of whatever happens now.'

Whatever happens? That was a recipe for international disaster if ever Ken had heard one.

'Do you think we should?'

She paused before answering him. 'What I think won't make any difference, Ken.' She called over a barman and persuaded him to bring them a bottle of rye even though he insisted it could only be served by the glass. Ken poured the drinks and Coraline slipped a ten-spot into the barman's pocket. He pretended not to notice. He pretended badly. They stared through the porthole, smoking and watching the stars running alongside the fuselage. 'Who are you, Ken?' She asked it thoughtfully, as if she really did want to know.

'Would you believe a farm boy from Georgia?'

'No, I wouldn't.' She drew a final line of silver smoke from her cigarette.

'It's who I am.'

'It's who you were,' she replied.

'Can't escape our past, Coraline.'

'Watch me.' And she pressed her cigarette stub into a gilded ashtray.

Brandies were being served and a fug of cigar smoke so

thick you could get lost in it for a week hung beneath the ceiling. At the end of the big seaplane was the 'honeymoon suite' – a fully private cabin, currently occupied by some European princeling and his 'friend', according to a whisper from their waiter during dinner. The suite might have seen a lot of people acting like it was their honeymoon, but very few of them wore wedding rings, the waiter added. He hung around until Coraline gave him a ten-spot too. It seemed to be the going rate.

Ken was looking forward to some time to rest, but his mind kept going back to the night he had spent at the Tookes' house, when the door to Coraline's room had been ajar. It had been interrupted by bloody events, but he had felt something powerful that evening and when he had entered her room, before he told her about Oliver, there had been a full four seasons in the way she had looked at him.

They stood beside their curtained miniature cabins now, not yet ready to part. 'This is all better than I had expected,' he said. 'I might just move in.'

'Better than your apartment?'

He laughed. 'In the way that Buckingham Palace is better than a muddy ditch.'

She paused. 'I looked something out for you.'

'What's that?'

An attendant brought her suede shoulder bag from the cloakroom. He didn't get a ten-spot for the trouble and looked disappointed. Coraline took a letter in a faded blue envelope from the side pocket. 'You can read it,' she said.

It was a letter on cream notepaper from her grandfather, Simeon.

Turnglass House, Ray, Essex
6th September, 1915

My dear Oliver, Alexander and Coraline,

I am old now and you have all your lives just beginning. To you, I'm a wrinkly old man, and what do children care for wrinkly old men? Nothing! And that is the way that it should be. You should care for fishing and playing in the trees and learning your school lessons. If only I could be your ages again! Well, that is all behind me now.

I am writing this letter while we are all together because I want you to remember me when I am long gone. Because I will remember you, wherever I am.

There was more about his wishes for them for the future, some advice about getting on with other people and the like. But one part of the letter stood out.

Coraline, one day you will be a fine young lady. But be careful not to be *too* ladylike. Your grandmother wasn't and she was a wonderful woman. So go up in those airplanes that your father raves about. Learn to fly one, even.

Alexander, I know you are going to be a leader of men. A soldier, I think. Maybe the navy for you. But I can see even at this age that you also have a good brain. An artist or writer would suit you well too.

Oliver. Oh, Oliver. I offer you my most profound apologies. You have such spirit and yet that body of

yours lets you down. I have done everything I can
think of, but I am writing this sitting in my usual seat,
watching you in your little glass room in the library,
hoping that I will have some flash of inspiration.

I know I won't.

You probably had no real idea what all those tests
and observations were about, but for these past
few months I have studied you in the wild hope on
your father's part – and mine – that I will come up
with some miracle to cure you of the effects of your
illness. But no, my dear grandson, nothing has shown
any promise. So I sit on the old sopha, watching you
playing with a toy bicycle, turning the wheels around
and around, and knowing that you will never get to
ride upon one. That is a great sadness to me and to
your father, who had such hopes for you, his first son.

'What does he mean, "your little glass room in the
library"?'

'My father had some idea that Simeon could find a cure
for the effects of Oliver's polio. It's not as outlandish as it
sounds – my grandfather's a doctor of infectious diseases
and had some renown for his work on treating cholera. We
were spending a year in England then. So Oliver had to
stay in isolation while my grandfather tried some things.
None of it worked, though he did eventually recover, as
you know.'

Ken checked the date on the letter. It was two months
before the abduction of Alexander. 'In Oliver's book—'

'You want to know about the glass box. In the story.'

So she had been reading it too. That glass chamber held such a central place in *The Turnglass*, it was astonishing to think it might also be true.

'I do.'

'Sure you do. Well, the truth is yes: I think that really happened. At least from what my grandfather told us.'

'Incredible.' Incredible that history had repeated – though this time, it was Simeon sitting on the sofa, watching day and night. 'Why did your parents go back there after your brother was abducted? I would have thought it would hold painful memories.'

'I expect it did. My parents and grandfather left it empty for years, but my father always said it was the ancestral home and ancestry should be revered.' She lifted an eyebrow sardonically in a way that told him ancestry, to her, counted for nothing. 'So they started returning each summer. Until my mother's death.' She looked over the letter again. 'Father lionizes Simeon. He often says, "your grandfather will be proud" – or disappointed, depending on what we've done. Anyway, I wanted you to read this so you know what my grandfather is really like, instead of getting it from Oliver's book.'

'I understand.'

There was a window beside her and the night sky seemed to be pouring through it. Maybe it was the rye or the heat, but he took half a step towards her. The lights above their heads were reflected in her milky blue irises. Her face turned up to his and he felt her breathing, slow and deep, as his hands lifted to her sides, drawing her closer. As he moved his mouth towards hers, her eyes seemed to lose their focus, looking right through him. And her lips turned away. She slowly shook her head, staring out at the night once more.

'Not now,' she said quietly. His hands dropped.

They stared at each other silently for a few seconds, each waiting for the other to move or the waiter to interrupt with a subtle cough or the plane to fall out the damn sky. Anything. There was nothing. She parted the curtains and let them fall back into place behind her.

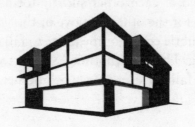

Chapter 11

They were woken in the mid-morning with thickly steaming coffee and tea. After washing and dressing, they emerged from the plane into the sunlight of an English summer. It was nothing at all compared to a California summer – it would, at best, have counted as spring to a Californian. Also, despite the luxury of the cabin, Ken hadn't rested well and his head was still full of the cigar-smoke fug from the previous evening. So the salty air of the Southampton harbour tingling the back of his throat perked him up, but did little to lift his mood.

As they made their way across the dockside, to be met by some puffed-up dignitary of the town and a senior

Pan Am employee, Ken looked around. This was the first sight he had had of Europe outside of newsreels, and it wasn't what he had expected. His image of the Old Country was a mix of mediaeval romance and Dickens novels. Half-forest, half-tumbling tenement. But here was a country gearing up to a twentieth-century war on land and sea: a vast warship was docked, and a swarm of tenders buzzed around it like wasps. In the harbour mouth, a minesweeper was chugging out to sea. Dark blue naval uniforms were all around, dotted with khaki army fatigues.

They look pretty resolved to what's going to happen, he noted. He hoped they could survive without help from the United States this time – if Governor Tooke got his way as President and kept American boys out of a second European theatre of slaughter.

Then they were catching trains and grimy London was passing in a blur. Ken was disappointed he wouldn't get to see this great capital, the source of the literary wine that he had drunk down during his lifetime. But at least there was countryside and genuine little villages with stone churches and maids on bicycles to watch as the train sped past. And finally, they were deposited in the town of Colchester in Essex – an ancient place built by the Romans, a faded sign at the station told them. It wasn't their final destination, but there was something Ken wanted to look into first.

'This is the nearest town, right?' he asked.

'To Ray? Yes, it is.'

'Then this would be where they held the coroner's court.'

'I suppose it would.'

An enquiry at the station ticket office directed them to a brick building no more than two streets away.

The clerk at the front desk replied that yes, anyone had the right to read court transcripts and if the gentleman would like to enter the third windowless room on the right, he would find them labelled by date.

'This one,' Coraline said, opening a wire-fronted wooden cabinet after they had searched for a while. She pulled out a heavy book bound in cheap card. It covered the year of her mother's death.

She laid it on an empty table and they read by the light of a single hanging bulb. British electric bulbs seemed to be far weaker than American versions.

> Death of Florence Tooke (Mrs). Inquest the seventh
> day of July, nineteen hundred and twenty.

Ken and Coraline read of the weather conditions that day – warm and bright – the testimony of a hatmaker who had attended her that morning and said that Florence had seemed happy enough, not at all, in her opinion, in the state of mind of a woman about to kill herself. There was the evidence of Governor Tooke, who said that yes, his wife had been unhappy since the disappearance of their son, but that her mind was quite balanced. But then there was the statement given by Florence's maid, Carmen, who was cleaning the Governor's study when, she said, she saw her mistress drop her easel and wade wildly out across the mudflats into the water, sinking down. Some local residents confirmed that others had died on the same ground. The file finished with the words:

Verdict: Open

And that, Ken knew, meant something suspicious. Something not quite right. He checked the door and quietly tore the pages from their binding, stuffing them inside his knapsack. 'No one else is going to want them,' he said.

'That's true.'

Outside, they took a few minutes in the late afternoon sunshine to think about what they had read.

'It was as Piers said,' Ken said, after a while. He had actually been half-expecting Bellen to have made it up.

'I was hoping it wouldn't be.'

'No, I can understand that.'

Up until that point, Florence's death had been simple. Painful, sure, but explained. And now Coraline was having to come to terms with the idea that both her brother and her mother had died in suspicious circumstances.

She and Ken said nothing more as they took a taxi from Colchester station out through low-lying boggy landscapes. This had been the Vikings' gateway to England, the cabbie informed them. Ken could see why: it was where the sea and land met and married. At times it was solid, at others it was a watery channel. Fields tipped into the freezing North Sea and islets reared up like ghosts.

Finally, the taxi drew up outside a pub. The sight

of it made Ken happy, because, while he might have missed the old London that he had dreamed about, here was an inn that had stood for four centuries and was still handing out weak beer served at room temperature. The sign was warped, but the name of the Peldon Rose was clear. The building was wide and low, with rough whitewashed walls that bowed out here and there with age.

The Peldon Rose had been described in Oliver's story. In it, the hero, the young Dr Simeon Lee, stepped from a coach that had stopped outside the pub on a blustery night towards the end of the nineteenth century, to peer into the murky events at his uncle's home, Turnglass House. Now, in the twentieth century, Ken stepped out of a cab with Simeon's ghost to investigate the death of Oliver at a California copy of that house.

'I'd forgotten this place,' Coraline said. She looked sick as she turned a circle, taking everything in, to end up facing an islet in front of them. That was Ray, the scene of Simeon Lee's investigation, the scene of Coraline's mother's death and Alex's disappearance. A few hundred yards long, it was low and squat like the runt of a litter. Beyond it rose another island, Mersea, where a small town clung onto the rocks.

Ken went to the window of the pub and peered in. He could see low oak beams and an inviting inglenook fireplace. A radio was playing something classical.

'Down from London, are you?' a hoarse voice rattled through the doorway.

Ken checked out his own clothes. They must have

been foreign enough to the locals. 'From a bit further than that!' he called out cheerfully, as he strode in to see a few patrons playing dominoes or sharing a newspaper at the bar.

The voice, it turned out, was attached to the landlord – a man thin as a rake – who was pouring beer from a jug for one of the newspaper-readers. Some of the drink slopped over the rim.

'You sound like it. You Americans?' He didn't sound pleased. The landlord in Oliver's book had been jollier.

'We are that,' Ken responded, in a genial attempt to raise the conversation's spirits. Coraline followed him in and glanced about like she was viewing her own coffin.

'First we've seen here in a while,' the landlord informed him. 'Had a Canadian last month, didn't we, Pete?' Pete, a nervous-looking soul in his forties or fifties with bright red hair, concurred. 'But they're different, aren't they?'

'They like to think so,' Ken confirmed. There was a pause as both parties ran out of road. 'Could we have two of those beers?' He was certain tepid beer in smeared glasses wasn't Coraline's drink of choice, but they couldn't get cute now. The radio continued with its lonely orchestra as they waited for the drinks to be served.

'Come for the oysters?' the barman enquired, seeming to wonder at visitors from so far away.

'We heard they were something special,' he lied.

The drinks were poured and they pushed a few pennies across the bar in return. As they did so, a woman – she looked about fifty and had buttoned up everything that could possibly have buttons – walked up to Pete and placed a single white feather in front of him. 'My boy's in the navy,' she said. 'Going up against the Nazis. You were a coward in the last one and you're a coward now. Same for all you lot. Fine church you have. Just cowards.' She stalked off and Pete, his cheeks reddened to the colour of his hair, quietly put the feather in his trouser pocket and pretended to read his part of the newspaper.

Ken returned to his conversation with the publican. 'Is there somewhere we can put up for a couple of nights?'

'A room? Well, yes, we have some here.' He spoke a little doubtfully. 'Fifteen shillings a night with meals. Ten without. Would that be one or . . .' his eyes undressed Coraline, '. . . two rooms?'

'Two.' Ken moved to block the man's line of vision. Sure, she wasn't actually his girl, but he wanted this guy to back off all the same.

The barman got the message.

After being shown to two rooms with all the comfort of a Trappist monastery and fewer of the amenities, they went downstairs. It was time to get down to business. The evening light was melting onto the roof and there was a smell of moist flowers in the air.

'We'd like to explore a little,' Ken told the publican. 'Those islands opposite. Can we get to them?'

The landlord looked up at the clock, then at a chart pinned to the wall. 'Not now. Tide's too high. The Strood – that's the path to them – it's covered up. Many's drowned trying to get across while the water's over it.' Ken felt Coraline bristle. 'It'll be dark before you can cross, so best to wait 'til tomorrow.'

Ken knew all about the tides over the Strood from *The Turnglass*, how they ebbed and flowed without mercy.

'We would rather go tonight, as soon as it's safe.'

The landlord shrugged his thin, bony shoulders. It was no skin off his nose if the local police would have to fish their bodies out of the mire twenty-four hours later. 'If you must.'

While they waited for the right time, they ate their evening meal. It featured, to Ken's disgust, a rubbery eel suspended in a cold and salty jelly, all presented on rough pureed potato. For form's sake, he forced it down, though it was more like swallowing an insult than food. Coraline didn't bother with form and picked at the potato before pushing the plate away.

'You don't need to tell me,' Ken said.

They kept up the pretence of being holidaymakers who had chosen a queer, out-of-the-way place for a visit by looking through a travel guide to eastern England that Ken had picked up at the railroad station. Eventually, the landlord checked the tide chart and his wristwatch and informed them that it would be safe enough to cross now, but did they have a torch to show them the way? No, Ken replied. The landlord huffed and reached under the counter for a battery-powered flashlight, which he tested and handed them. The ruinous hire of it would be added to their bill.

'Straight down the Strood, then. That takes you onto Ray, then Mersea. Mersea town's on the west side. Won't

GARETH RUBIN

be much to see at this time, though.' Well, there probably wouldn't be so much more in daylight.

The Strood was a narrow causeway out to the two islets, which were cut off from the mainland by wide creeks. The slippery narrow path was perhaps a hundred yards long from the mainland onto Ray. It ran across Ray for the same distance, and then onto Mersea. At low tide, it was no more than three feet above the lapping waves through the channels, and by the torchlight Ken could see the water rising up to snatch at the road and anyone on it.

As he walked, he knew he was walking literally in the footsteps of Simeon, the hero of *The Turnglass*. That crazy story. From Coraline's information, the tale was all based on the experience of Oliver's grandfather in the 1880s, although it was hard to say how much of the book was history and how much was the product of Oliver's imagination.

Ray itself was a low, flat bully of an island. Its brow jutted over the sea in a bad-tempered challenge. What life it supported was similar: spiky plants grabbing onto the salty soil and a few screeching birds that didn't stay longer than it took to declare the triangular island barren.

Barren apart from a house that stood slate-black against the inky sky.

'That's it,' Coraline said. Ken turned the torch's powerful beam on the building.

Turnglass House, where, in the story, Simeon Lee had disinterred a secret with his bare hands, dragging it out of the mud. And where, in this world, Oliver's brother and mother had both disappeared. The house sat at the southern point of the islet, flanked by mud-flats to the east. It would have been a good place to go quietly insane.

Coraline's voice changed as the beam lit it. She sounded confused. 'What's happened to it?'

It was a good question. A house needs glass in the windows, doors in the walls and a roof. This pile of ordered bricks seemed to reach up and up, but on top of its blackened walls there were only patches of timber and tiles, while its windows were empty.

'A fire,' Ken said. Black scorch marks above the windows were just visible in the torchlight.

'I had no idea.' They stared at the ruin. 'So when my father comes, this is what he sees.'

'This is what he sees,' Ken repeated.

Moving off again, wary, as if the fire was somehow waiting out of sight to rush them, they wound along a tramped-down path that was just visible through the tough vegetation. 'If it was empty at the time, that means someone burned it deliberately,' Ken said when they were ten yards from the open doorway. 'Either that or it was struck by lightning, but that's a one in a million chance.'

'Don't write it off. We Tookes have strange luck.' Well, recent events had proved her right on that score.

They reached the entrance, and Ken tugged the bell-pull. Even though his brain told him not to, he expected to hear the same ringing that Simeon had heard. But there was no sound, of course. And anyhow the door that had swung open for Simeon was now just a few chunks of oak held by rusted hinges. It all looked like a beat-up rear-guard after a disastrous battle that everyone wanted to forget.

Inside, the torchlight fell on charred, overturned furniture: a huge porter's chair, a long rosewood table that must once have been very fine, an iron fireplace. The floor was Victorian black-and-white chequer, inlaid with a delicate design of stars but mostly covered by dirt. A musty smell reeked from the house's gizzard.

Coraline went first, treading through scattered soil and splinters. Her feet clipped on the floor. Something in the dark recesses scuttled away. 'So, this is your inheritance,' Ken said.

'Like I said: we Tookes have strange luck.'

Further in was a small sitting room, with a wide hole burned right through the floorboards. 'This must have been where it started,' Ken told her. The wood panelling on the walls had been turned into fuel. There were a few shards of glass inside the room where the windows had exploded with the heat. The iron frames remained. Ken thought again of the story set between these walls. He could see the sick Parson Hawes shuffling through. But what shadows now hid in its corners? Had Oliver found something when he had come to England, something that had led to his death?

'Where are you going?'

Ken had started down a corridor to the rear. He paused underneath a scorched painting hanging skew-whiff on the wall. A hunting scene.

'The kitchen's this way.'

'How do you . . .' She broke off. 'Of course. That damn story.' The torch beam glittered in her eyes.

The kitchen had a huge cast-iron cooking range that could probably have worked as well now as the day it was delivered. 'Stove's bigger than my apartment,' Ken said. There was nothing else there except memories held by the dead. 'Let's go upstairs.' It was time to approach the true heart of the house.

They retraced their steps to the hallway and stared up to the floor above, over which the night clouds hung and a few screeching gulls flitted. A wide wooden staircase led up. Despite the fire, it was mostly intact. They picked their way through a maze of cracks and holes in the timber. A light drizzle began to fall, soaking into the floorboards.

'I had forgotten how insane the proportions of this place are,' Coraline said as they reached the top.

'What do you mean?'

'It's like our house in California. From the outside, it looks like there are three storeys. But there's only actually two. This upper one is just incredibly tall,' Coraline said, her words becoming damp in the air. Ken let the torchlight play up to the top line of bricks and the last vestiges of the roof. 'I wonder why you build a house like that.'

'To get more light in, presumably.' He looked up at the void that was once the roof. 'Well, someone succeeded.'

And then the torch beam fell on something that had fallen from the roof: a man-sized wrought iron bracket that held a huge glass weather vane in the shape of an hourglass. The glass was broken in two. No sands would ever flow from one half to the other.

'The house was named after that,' Coraline said. 'I guess the name means nothing now.'

They stepped over wooden joists, along the landing that spanned the upper floor, to a door that still sported some charred green leather. Ken guessed what was on the other side. It was the source of the mystery in Oliver's story, the spring from which all else flowed. He pushed at the door, but it was warped and stiff in its frame. He put his shoulder to it, but it still wouldn't budge. 'I'm going to have to bust it in,' he said. He handed Coraline the flashlight, took a step back and charged at the door with all his weight. It held out for a fraction of a second before giving up and breaking in two. And there he saw it all, just as Oliver's story had described: a thousand or more books lining the tall walls of the library. There was one elemental difference between the novel and the sight itself, though, because in the story, they were fine and revered volumes stretching across the range of human learning; but here they were scorched by fire, covered in lichen and caked in a lifetime of dirt. It wasn't a library, it was a morgue for books. And each one was a John Doe.

Ken looked to the end of the room, wondering just what he might find. The beam followed, as Coraline had the same thought. It fell on a void: a dry, ashen expanse without books, shelves or furniture. No eyes silently glittering. All that was left of that observation chamber was a pile of exploded glass on the floor, malevolently reflecting the room in a hundred broken images. That chamber had once meant something terrible: the imprisonment of sickness and despair. Now those ghosts had been set free.

Ken checked a line of books, running his finger along their spines. He must have been in the natural sciences section, because there were tomes that explained chemical reactions and described frogs in South America. He neatly replaced them among the wreckage. Even he didn't know why he took the trouble when he could have thrown them in any direction and it wouldn't have made a blind bit of difference to the scene.

'What did you think we would find?' Coraline asked.

'Not this. This is a surprise,' he replied. 'It's eerie to be here after reading about it. But the fire? Yeah, that was unexpected.'

It would only ever be a home now for the birds and whatever creatures were skulking in the corners. But the question was whether Oliver had found something else when he had come, something that had started him on a track to his own destruction. From his knapsack, Ken pulled his copy of *The Turnglass*, and read, by torchlight, a passage about the room that stood around them.

He called for Peter Cain. The man came with his hands filthy and a shovel in his grip. 'I been buryin' that dead foal. No use fer lame animals. Wan' ter help me dig him in?' he said insolently. Simeon sent him to bring Watkins immediately, and then went up to the library. Florence was sitting at the small octagonal table, upon which sat the little glass model of the house that held them all, its three human figurines waiting behind the coloured doors of the upper floor like actors ready to play their parts. There was a fire in the grate, and the light of its

red flames danced across the yellow silk dress Simeon
had picked out for her. She sang a snatch from the hymn
once more, '*Help of the helpless, oh, abide with me.*'

Florence. With his story, Oliver had given his mother life
beyond the one cut short in the real world. She lived on in
the play-scene he had created. It was sad to read.

There was nothing else to see, so they tried the other
doors on the landing. Two rooms were bare apart from
beds rotted to sticks by the rain. The final door was stiff,
but gave way without the need to charge it down, which
saved Ken's shoulder another beating.

'This was my father's study when we were here,'
Coraline said, peering in like she must have done as a girl.
'I remember standing in the doorway and watching him
working. There.' A roll-top secretaire and a high-backed
wooden chair dominated the room. The desk had been
sheltered by a lonely surviving patch of roof and had been
untouched by flames. It was the widow at a funeral that
no one else was attending.

An astronomical panorama carved into the desk was
as bold as it had ever been, but when Ken looked through
the drawers – which turned out to be difficult because
the wood had buckled so he had to wrench them out – he
found it completely empty.

There was little more to examine – some upturned
boxes and a bank of shelves whose entire manifest read:
one cracked vase, a small ceramic box and a pile of mouse
droppings. Ken sat in the tall chair and sighed. But then
his eye fell on something: one of the drawers had refused

to push all the way back in. He had thought it was the damaged wood, but it could be something else. He pulled the drawer right out and felt around in the cavity. Yes, there! Right at the back, there was something there. He closed it in his fingers and drew it out.

It was an oval object, two inches long and made of china. Its two halves, which opened like an oyster, were decorated with gilt and delicate curving lines of mother-of-pearl. Someone had paid a good chunk of money for this.

'I know what it is,' Coraline told him the second it appeared in the light.

But Ken wasn't waiting to be informed. He prised the two halves apart and found himself looking at a pair of miniature paintings, done in delicate touches of watercolour that must have taken a tiny sable brush. One was of the house in which they stood, seen from a distance under an evening sky and before the fire that had remodelled it without a deal of care. Its pair, set upside down, was of the house's namesake on a cliff face in California, in broad daylight.

'Tell me,' Ken said.

'My mother painted them sometimes. I have one. This must be Oliver's. I don't know why he put it here.'

No, that was the boulder of a question.

'Maybe so it was with your mother. In a way.' He was far from convinced that was the answer.

'It's possible.'

So, the room had held a secret all right. But it wasn't something that Oliver had discovered; it was something he had left.

Coraline looked out of the room's only window, which faced due south. Ken followed her line of sight down to the muddy shore at the tip of the islet, just visible in the moonlight. 'I want to leave,' she said. 'There's nothing else here.' Nothing but bad memories, she could have added for accuracy.

She walked away, towards the stairs. Ken followed, but something occurred to him and he stopped. He reached into his knapsack and this time pulled out the coroner's inquest minutes that he had torn from their bindings.

'Wait,' he said.

'Why?'

'There *is* something here.' He flicked through the report. 'Yes, here.' He stabbed his forefinger at the page. He read at double speed the words where Governor Tooke had said his wife had been suffering no mental imbalance on the morning of her death, and where the hatmaker who had visited had said Florence Tooke had seemed happy enough. Then to her maid's evidence. 'Look. Carmen's statement to the court.'

'So?'

'Stay here. I'm going out onto the mudflats.'

'What?'

'I'm going to signal to you with the flashlight. Shout when you see the signal.' At that, he rushed out, leaving her in the room lit only by weak moonlight.

With the torch, he picked out his route down the stairs and out the front door. He shone the beam onto his footway. The ground grew soggier, slopping up the sides of his legs. He slowed, knowing exactly what could happen if he stumbled onto the wrong patch, maybe dropped the flashlight, got sucked down . . .

To hell with that. He'd been through too much to go the same way as Florence. He was coming through this, finding what had happened to Oliver and taking it out on whoever had blood on his hands.

And then the ground was more freezing mud than soil. The electric light fell on a brown expanse that could be the shoreline or a dirty sea. Three more steps and his feet sank. One more to be sure. And he was up to his knees in mud. He couldn't risk another. And he turned to the house. He waved the torch left to right, right to left. Then up and down in a holy cross. 'Coraline!' he shouted. The sound echoed, even though there didn't seem to be a single thing for it to bounce off. It was bouncing off desolation. He waved and shouted again.

And then he heard her voice, very distant.

'Yes!'

He waved the cross once more, pulled his numb feet from the mud and stole back to the house. Up through the hall, leaving a filthy trail to the study.

'What did you see?' he asked as soon as he caught sight of her, sitting in the window.

'Nothing.'

Exactly what he expected her to see. 'I thought so. Carmen told the court that she was in here when she saw your mother wade across the mudflats. Quite a trick when the window faces the other direction.' Coraline pursed her lips. 'Tell me about Carmen,' said Ken.

'She's been with us for my whole life.'

Well, that meant she knew more family secrets than a room full of their lawyers and bankers. 'We need to speak to her when we get back. Do you trust her?'

There was a pause. 'Who can you really trust?'

Yeah, that was true.

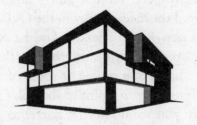

Chapter 12

'I wonder what they do around here for entertainment of an evening,' Ken said as they sat in the corner of the Rose.

'Slaughter a cow, bury themselves alive. Don't ask me.'

Coraline had to be feeling pretty cut up about the lies that were being uncovered. 'Is there anything you want to do to take your mind off things?'

'Like what?'

'Cards? Or I think they play cribbage here.'

'What is that?'

'Something with matchsticks, I think.'

'So neither of us knows how to play it.'

'No. Gin rummy?'

She shrugged in acceptance. Ken borrowed a deck

of cards from the landlord and dealt. They attracted a small crowd of locals, who asked them how to play and then joined in. By the end, they were part of the regular crowd at the inn and everyone treated Ken as a pal and Coraline with respect. He felt guilty about it, but Ken actually enjoyed those few hours in the Old Country with her and their new-found friends. And he could tell that the flickering fire in the grate and their jostling mates had warmed her a little. She smiled at some of the jokes and drank something near to a pint of the pub's gin. It was so watered-down you would need a barrel to get anywhere near drunk, but Ken suspected even the full-strength stuff would have barely touched her.

In the night, he woke with a start. But his dream still flooded his vision: Coraline in the red bathing costume she had worn on Oliver's boat the day they had all been carefree on the ocean. Only this time his fingers weren't handing her a cocktail, they were reaching for the laces that tied her costume at the back. The laces unfurled themselves like snakes and curled around his wrists, binding him.

In the dark of his bedroom, he could feel his chest heaving and his hands stretching out.

'Jesus Christ,' he muttered to himself.

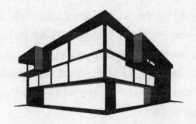

Chapter 13

Ken woke properly before eight. It was too early for break-fast to be served so he took out Oliver's book and began to re-read the story, taking time over it. There was a hell of a lot more to it than lay on the surface, that was for sure. He found himself thinking about how the Simeon character discovered a novel called *The Gold Field* about a Californian travelling to England to find the truth about his mother. It was a reflection of Oliver's own quest; that was a no-brain deduction for anyone who knew his family history. Yeah, Oliver's book was a message to those he had left behind.

Ken read it line by line, checking every word like it

was new in case he missed something, while the sound of the publican sweeping up and shifting chairs around drifted up from the pub below. And when he came to the description of Simeon's first days in the house on Ray, something chimed in his brain. He flicked back and forth looking for a passage about the servants at the house. Then he found it. It was an echo on the page of something he had heard in real life, something he had heard said in the pub. He snapped the book shut, let out a laugh and thumped it down on his bed before hurrying to Coraline's room.

'Come downstairs with me,' he said. 'There's someone we need to meet.'

She checked her wristwatch. 'Is it the mailman?'

'Just come.' They descended to the tap room. The landlord was sharing a dirty story with a barman who was helping him set the place straight, and didn't bother cutting it short when he saw Coraline. 'There was a man here last night,' Ken said, when the tale was over. 'Red hair. His name was Pete.'

'Pete Weir?' the landlord said warily.

'If you say so. He's a Quaker, isn't he? Conscientious objector.'

'How d'you know that?' He sounded even more than before like he wasn't keen on anyone asking questions, let alone Americans who claimed to have come for the oysters, which was about as believable as them claiming to have come for the scenery.

'That woman gave him a white feather, and she was talking about his church being cowards.'

'He's a Quaker, aye,' the barman relented. 'Nothing wrong with that.'

A fine Quaker who frequented pubs, but Ken wasn't going to make a point of it. He rapped on the bar, pleased at the confirmation because this might just send them on a trail that led somewhere, instead of just-about-nowhere like the others they had followed so far. 'We'd like to speak to him.'

'What about?'

'Nothing important.' The landlord's eyebrows were eloquent in their scepticism. 'Where could I find him?'

The man wiped down the grimy wooden counter thoughtfully, deciding whether it was safe to share the information with outsiders who were here for some reason that really wasn't an out-of-the-way vacation. 'His house is down on the Hard. On Mersea.'

'Thanks. How will I know which one?'

'Got a sign outside offering oysters for sale.' Ken thanked him again and the landlord looked at the barman. The other man shrugged, as if the ways of Americans were always hard to understand. Ken was making for the door when the landlord called out, 'He won't be there now.'

'No?'

'Out on his boat, harvesting. Oysters don't just walk out of the sea and into pots.'

'I'm sure. Do you know when he'll be back?'

'Four or five, probably.'

That was frustrating, but there was little to be done. 'Okay. Thank you.'

The barman nodded in reply.

'What's this all about?' Coraline asked, taking Ken aside.

'There's a servant in the book,' he explained. 'Peter Cain. He's a red-haired Quaker who knocks back the drink. Just like Pete Weir. It's quite a coincidence – too much, I think. Maybe Oliver did it consciously, maybe it was unconscious, but he put Pete Weir in *The Turnglass*. We need to find out what he has to say. We'll see when he gets back.'

So they ate their breakfast of mackerel and heavy bread. Then they returned to Turnglass House. It looked better by day, but not by much.

'The fire really did a number on it,' Ken said.

'I wish it had been knocked down.'

It was true that the house was crying out for a bulldozer more than anything else. They explored again, the daylight illuminating more than the flashlight they had had the previous night, but they found nothing more of use and left empty-handed.

Half an hour later, they had padded their way right across Ray and onto its sibling, Mersea. Mersea had a few shrubs and trees, which made it look like a garden paradise compared to scrub-faced Ray. The ground lifted higher above sea level, too, making it large enough to pretend it was a small town. There were a couple of churches, a short street of sad shops and the beach – the Hard, as the locals called it, as if another syllable would have killed them. It was a shingly stretch, deep enough to land fishing boats, with a natural harbour that had been reinforced with a breakwater.

A number of fishermen's cottages stood on the seafront, where men were hurrying to and fro with pots and nets. A few of the houses had boards outside offering wares, but only one was advertising oysters: a single-storey weather-boarded building. This was Pete Weir's, but no one was home, as the pub landlord had told them to expect.

What to do to kill time? They weren't spoiled for choice, and so opted for walking about the town, looking into the churches, watching the fishing boats come and go and trying Weir's cottage from time to time without success. 'I grew up by the ocean,' Coraline said, sitting on a concrete bench. 'I found it comforting. Not so much now.'

'I can understand that.'

When late afternoon rolled in, they decided it was time to call on Weir again.

'Are you sure about this?' Coraline asked.

'What do you mean?'

'I mean, you're attaching a lot of importance to a detail in Oliver's book.'

He had been thinking a lot about that book, even while they had sat on the seafront watching the boats unload their catches.

'They call it a *roman à clef*: a novel with a key. The book itself unlocks the truth. And I only just realized something else.'

'Which is?'

'That the "enquiries agent" character – I suppose that's a detective to us – calls himself Cooryan when he wants an alias. I can only guess that's meant to be my surname. I think Oliver left it as a sign to me in case something happened to him. He wanted me to let people know the truth if he couldn't himself.'

She sat for a moment, considering it. 'You think he knew what was coming?' she asked.

'I think he knew it was a possibility. How does that make you feel?'

She stared out to sea. 'Responsible.'

This time, when they approached the little fisherman's cottage, the curtain had been drawn back from the window. Through a cracked pane, Ken could see Pete Weir at a tiny table in a corner, nursing a glass of milk and a plate of pickled fish. It was a single room with a few matchsticks of furniture and an area curtained off to create a sleeping space. Weir was pushing the fish around with his fork, no appetite on show. Ken tapped on the window – afraid it might cave in – and the man jerked up, looking left and right, amazed at the interruption to his routine. Gingerly he beckoned them to enter.

The room smelled powerfully of the sea. 'It's Pete, isn't it?' The man nodded, a little suspicious. He wasn't a man people sought out. 'My name is Ken Kourian. Would it be all right if I asked you something?' Weir grunted something that was probably an agreement. 'Thanks. Tell me, have you lived on Mersea all your life?' He grunted again. 'That's something. Where we come from, people are always moving. It must be fine to have a home and know it's your home.'

'It is, Mister Kourian.' Weir seemed confused by the strange name and pronounced it very carefully. But it appeared that few people chatted to him, and he was settling a bit now, so was keen to keep up some conversation. 'Are you here on honeymoon?' Coraline burst out laughing. Ken stifled a smile. Weir looked bewildered. 'I'm sorry, Mrs Kourian. Have I . . . ?'

'Miss Tooke,' she said.

His face fell. After a moment, his jaw opened and moved as if masticating. 'Miss . . .'

'Tooke. Coraline Tooke. The name means something to you.' Weir looked about the room, seemingly worried that someone had overheard. 'Yes, I can see it does.'

'What does it mean to you?' Ken stepped in. 'Pete?'

The man stretched leathery fingers towards his drink, then thought better of it and withdrew his hand. Ken wondered if there was more in the glass than milk alone. 'I worked for your family,' he mumbled.

'Do you remember me?' Coraline asked. He shrugged, as if that would let him off the hook. 'I think you do.' She paused. 'Do you remember my brother Oliver?' At that, Weir's eyelids lifted, then fell again. 'He's been here, hasn't he?' Another moment of dead air between them. 'What did he say?'

'Pete? Please tell us.'

Silence for an age. Then he broke it. 'Asked me about your ma.'

Ken felt a jolt. There it was, the fork in the road that would take them from 'nowhere' to 'somewhere'.

'What about her?' Coraline demanded. This time, Weir's hardened fingers made it all the way to the glass and he tipped what remained into his mouth. 'Pete?'

'Please. I don't want to be involved.'

Ken met Coraline's glance. He was about to speak when she put her hand in her pocket and drew out her purse. She unclipped it and drew out a five-pound note. She placed it on the table. It was probably a week's earnings for Weir. He sighed.

Five pounds was all it took. It would probably have taken much less. 'Not what he said, is it? It's what I said. What I saw.'

The truth was in sight now.

'And what was that?'

'Shouldn't say.'

'I think you have to now,' Ken told him.

Weir nervously rolled the glass in his fingers. 'It was after they said she drowned.' He briefly looked up to Coraline, then dropped his gaze, ashamed. 'The day after.'

'What was?' Ken demanded.

'I was in the Rose.'

'So?' Ken tried to hurry him to the point.

'A car arrived outside. Big car. Didn't recognize it.'

'Go on.'

And then the punch. 'I saw the mistress's maid, Carmen, carrying some things to it.'

Ken started to comprehend. 'What sort of things?'

'Dresses. The mistress's dresses. Other things. Her vanity set. Not everything she owned. Just the essentials.' And his eyes went to Coraline's for the last time. 'If she'd drowned, where were they going? Tell me that.'

Tell me that. Ken thought of Governor Tooke's continued visits to England and looked to the daughter of a drowned woman who still needed her clothes. A woman whose body had never washed up on the shallow coastline. A woman whose loyal maid had lied to a coroner's court about witnessing her death.

'She's alive,' Coraline breathed.

And Ken thought of the part that Florence's dresses played in Oliver's novel too, bringing her back to a semblance of life. Perhaps Oliver had thought about his mother's gowns so much that they had made it onto the page.

'I've thought about it a lot,' the leathery man muttered to himself.

'I've thought about it more,' Coraline told him.

'Did you ever tell anyone? Speak to anyone?' Ken asked.

'Never said a word.' He sounded truly remorseful. 'Family business. Didn't seem my place. 'Til your brother came asking.'

Ken probed more, but the man told him nothing else of use. In the end, they went out into the late Mersea afternoon.

'Where is she?' Coraline asked as they walked back.

'I don't know. I think Oliver did. But look. Your father came once a year. He wasn't visiting the place of her death, he was visiting her alive. So we presume it's still in England – London, probably, so he could get there easily. And she's being held there, we also presume.' And once again he thought of the book. He pulled it from his jacket pocket and thumbed the pages. He knew the chapter he needed. It detailed a hunt through London, an incarceration and a secret revealed.

'But it's true. And a few days later, Nathaniel brought me what I was looking for. It was an address in St George's Fields in Southwark.'

St George's Fields. He understood immediately. Yes, he had seen that place himself and had sympathy for any who resided there. 'I can guess the address you mean.'

'I thought you might. Well, Nathaniel asked me if I knew about these places. I told him that I had read about them, but never thought I would be visiting one. "No, miss, not many do."'

'And yet, the very next day, I was in a Hansom heading for it.'

Simeon interrupted. 'The Magdalen Hospital for the Reception of Penitent Prostitutes,' he said. 'You don't forget that name.'

'You don't. So, there I was before this large brick building that looked much like a prison.'

'Ken, are you telling me . . .'

'I don't know. The name is insane, but I don't know if the place is real or if Oliver made it up entirely. It's worth trying.'

'How?'

'Well, they must have a telephone number information system in this country.'

They hurried back to the pub, where the landlord pointed him to a telephone in the corner. It was probably the only one for miles around. Coins fell in the slot and Coraline watched Ken speak into the receiver, wait a few seconds, speak again and then hold for a while before apparently thanking whoever was on the other end and hanging up. 'No listing for that name in London. But it might well have a different name.'

'So?'

'So we can't get there tonight, but tomorrow we go to London and we hunt for it.'

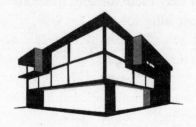

Chapter 14

They were discussing the journey to London over their breakfast mackerel when the landlord casually struck up conversation. 'So, what did you want to speak to Pete about?'

Ken didn't want everyone knowing. 'Nothing in particular,' he said, attempting to dead-end the talk.

'Wasn't about the Tookes, then?'

Ken swallowed his mouthful of fish. There was no point attempting to evade the issue. 'Yes, it was.'

'And you're Miss Tooke, then?' the landlord coolly threw to Coraline. She blinked in agreement, though Ken thought the look on her face right then could have beaten down a marine.

At this, the landlord decided to join them at their table. 'I remember your family well,' he said. 'My dad worked for them a bit here 'n' there. Grandad too, now I think of it.' He stroked his chin with a damp hand. 'Handsome woman, your ma.' He paused. 'Pity, that. All about your brother, wasn't it?'

The man was subtle as a quart of cheap whiskey. 'It might have been,' Ken said. 'We're here to find out what we can.'

'Find out? You're raking all that up?'

'We're raking all that up,' Coraline confirmed.

The landlord went to the bar, where he reached for a couple of plates, a thoughtful expression on his face. 'Know about Charlie White, do you?'

Know about him? Charlie White appeared as a brutal twenty-year-old in *The Turnglass*. The fates of his cousins, John and Annie, were central to the story. It was easy to forget sometimes that the events in the book were based on what had happened to Oliver's grandfather almost sixty years earlier. Were those events connected to what had happened to the family in 1915? At this point, Ken was ready to bet his shirt on it. 'Yes, I do,' Ken said.

'Charlie was *spoken to* about ... what was his name? Alex?'

'Who by?' Ken asked, although he was getting the idea.

'By the constables.'

'Why?'

The publican addressed Coraline. 'He was seen about your house when your brother went missing. No reason to be there. Said he went for a walk. Who goes for a walk on Ray? Reeks, if you ask me.' He settled against the bar. 'But who'm I to say? It was long ago.'

'Is he alive? Does he still live here?'

'Charlie White's going nowhere but Hell,' the landlord muttered in response. 'I'd stay away if I was you.'

'Not a chance.'

The landlord sighed. 'No. Well, he must be nigh-on eighty now. Last I heard of him, he was holed up with Mags Protheroe. He's got a nice little cottage on Mersea.'

If Charlie White's little cottage had ever been 'nice', those days had been lost in time. It was a gap-toothed hovel, at least half the windows were missing and the front door had been kicked in and badly boarded together. More than once, by the look of it.

As they approached the door, a foul cooking smell burst out, closely followed by a woman in her sixties with a dirty linen cap. She glared at the approaching couple.

'Who the twist are you?' she shrieked.

'We're looking for Charlie White.' Ken's accent or tone stopped her dead and she stared at him, then the cottage.

'What for?'

Ken took that to be as good an invitation as they were going to get, and marched up to the door. 'Charlie White?' he called.

A man who had once been huge but now had the skin hanging down on him lurched into the doorway, scowling and spitting by turns. 'Do I know you?' he demanded.

Charlie White was no intellectual giant, but there was animal cunning in his face. It would be better, Ken thought, to be upfront. He said who they were. The cunning look deepened and White's mouth opened to reveal a drunken line of thick teeth.

'How can I be of service?' he sneered.

It was Coraline who answered. 'The police spoke to you about my brother's disappearance. Why?'

'Why not? I was in the "v'cinity", as they put it. Long time ago, girly.'

'Did you see anyone there? Anyone suspicious?'

'Not a stoat.' He crossed his arms. He was enjoying himself.

'What did the police say?'

'Have to ask thems, won't you?'

'They're probably dead by now.'

'Let's hope.'

'You must know something.'

'Know lots've things. Don't mean I'll tell you 'em.'

'Why were you there?'

But White didn't answer that question. Instead, he leaned on the door frame and sneered. 'You know what? I've just thought of something. You never lived here. Never have. So everything you heard about all that, you heard from him.'

'From who?'

He chewed the name like it was cheap tobacco. 'Simeon Tooke.' He watched them beadily as he paused. 'What do you really know about your grandad, then, girly? I mean, *really* know?'

'A lot more than you do.'

He laughed. 'Yeah? Well, then I'm the one to tell you something about him.'

'Go on.'

'He was a swindler.' His face split into the closest thing to a smile that he could muster. 'You know he always wanted that house?' He pointed in the direction of Ray. 'That's what I was told any road. Played there as a boy, set his sights on it as a man. Got it by hook or by crook, they say. By hook *or by crook*. Bumped off his uncle or cousin or what-have-you to get his hands on it, they say. Didn't care who got roughed up along the way, who got made poor.'

Coraline's eyes narrowed. It was a hell of a revelation – if that's what it was. But either way, it was nothing like Oliver's story. 'Who do you mean "got roughed up"?' Ken asked.

'Who?' He chewed the invisible tobacco again. 'Me cousin John. You heard've him?'

Coraline spoke. 'It was my grandfather who found him.'

'Yeah, yeah. Funny that. Him being right there at the right time. Find someone where he found John? Funny that, wasn'it?'

'Are you saying he had something to do with it? He didn't even know your cousin.'

'Didn't he? He said he didn't. How do we know that's true?' White's expression darkened further. 'Now, I've had enough of this. Shog off.' He pulled open his filthy jerkin to show the wooden hilt of a knife tucked inside his belt.

*

They talked it over as they made their way back to the pub. It was all getting as murky as the sea around Ray. Just what had Oliver turned up? What had he been trying to tell people? So many family secrets: Alex, Florence, Oliver, Simeon. But then, they might all be the same secret. That was an idea to pitch and catch.

As they entered the Rose, the landlord beckoned them over. 'Tell me something,' he said. 'You got friends around here?'

'Friends?' asked Ken. 'No.' And already he didn't like the way this conversation was heading.

'Right.' The barman crossed his arms. 'Only someone's been asking.'

'About us?'

'That's right. Sounded like a Yank too. Come in an hour ago, asking if his pals were staying because he's lost the name of the pub they're in. Cock 'n' bull story. Only one pub round here for miles. I told him I've never heard of you. Dunno if he believed me, but he went off again.'

'What did he look like?' Ken had a damn good idea what the guy looked like.

The landlord shrugged. 'Brown hair. Tall as me, I suppose. Ordinary-lookin'.'

'And he asked for us by name?'

'Yeah.'

Ken took Coraline aside. It was bad news. Yeah, it sounded a lot like the man who had pushed him onto the tracks before they caught the airplane.

'What do we do?' she asked.

'Stick with the plan and head straight to London.'

So they took a cab to Colchester and the train on to London, taking a few things with them in case they stayed overnight. It buzzed again and again in Ken's mind that they were retracing the steps of Florence in *The Turnglass*. When they pulled into Liverpool Street Station, he could almost see a venal little postmaster, his palm itching for coins, and a dark-clad parson descending from the train.

They continued in her footsteps, taking a cab to St George's Fields in Southwark – the area still existed, though it had been grossly changed by time and not for the better. There weren't many fields in St George's Fields now, only a pile of dirty streets stalked by buses and underfed children with faces like executioners. Incongruously, something musical was playing in the air and Ken couldn't help humming the holy and hopeful words without even noticing it.

Coraline spotted it, though. 'What are you doing?' she asked.

He realized what he was doing. A tuneful chime of church bells had reminded him of a song and it had taken hold of his brain. 'Nothing. Let's ask around.' The first person they asked – a lad selling fruit from a cart – had never heard of the Magdalen Hospital for the Reception of Penitent Prostitutes. In fact, he sniggered at the name and leered at Coraline, which earned him a few harsh phrases from Ken. A few more passers-by, a housewife counting her change outside a tobacconist's, a drunk leaning against a shop door, a girl dragging a mangy-looking dog, were unhelpful; and as they asked the last one, Ken noticed the music on the air again – the same church clock was striking each quarter hour with a single bar of music.

They took a break in a corner coffee house. Something called 'tea cakes' – which were little more than toasted

bread with a few lonely raisins dropped in as decoration –
were brought alongside weak coffee. They sipped the
drink and chewed the food. They didn't speak, wary that
it might bring on bad luck for their quest. And then they
were back out on the street, asking questions of people
who looked at them as if they were insane. An angry
couple, an old woman who didn't know what day it was,
a family who apologised for having no clue. A man who
burst into laughter and what sounded like Greek, a couple
more shaken heads and then, finally, a bow-legged old
man who knew something.

'That's it. Was it,' he announced in an accent that it was
a wonder anyone could understand. He was pointing at
a set of eighteenth-century buildings. 'Not no more now.
Now it's 'omes. Been like that fifty year'more.' The work-
house of Oliver's story had been turned into apartments
half a century earlier. Coraline's mother could hardly be
there. Yet another dead end.

'Did it move?' Coraline asked.

'Move? The 'ospital?'

'Yes.'

The man stroked his chin. 'Now I think of't, it did,
yeah, it did. But it changed 's well.'

'How?'

'Become a school. Girls' school. Changed its name, of
course.' Well, that could hardly have been a tough debate.
'Moved to Streatham, I fink.'

Coraline swore in exasperation. Her mother couldn't
be there either.

Ken was listening to the exchange, but part of his mind

was somewhere else. That part had fixed on the melody in the air. Yes, it was a ringing of bells. He heard the words in his mind to match them. '*Help of the helpless, oh, abide with me …*' And the words began to crawl out onto his lips. Coraline stared at him. He ignored her and sang more of the tune. Then he lifted his head and listened. The tune was around them. No, it was coming from that road in front. But it wasn't just any song, it was the hymn that Florence sang to herself over and over in Oliver's story as she heard church bells chime it. And it was being chimed now by church bells close by.

'This way!' he shouted, charging into the next road. The tune would end soon. It was the final quarter hour being struck by the church clock. Coraline threw a look at him that said he had lost his mind, but followed him.

Ken ran twenty paces, then stopped sharp, listening hard. The tune was in its last notes. He turned right and ran into a narrow street populated only by an old couple hugging and crying. The melody died as he looked up and down the street. 'Where the hell is it coming from?' he demanded of Coraline as she appeared in the mouth of the street.

'What?'

'The …' and then his prayers were answered as the same bells chimed the hour itself: twelve strikes. He rode them through a dank passageway into another street. And then, finally, he saw the building. 'There. She's in there.'

At the end of the road, iron gates shut off a small estate. Yellow honeysuckle was climbing out over the walls and an old metal plate on the wall said it was the Convent

Hospital of the Sisters of St Agnes of Jerusalem. The place had an air like it was waiting to wake from a dream.

Through the wrought iron, Ken saw a sprawling building thrown together in a mish-mash of different styles. At least it looked well kempt. He wondered what Coraline was thinking as she saw it all, knowing that her mother was probably inside. Back from the dead, if not actually back to life.

Like Turnglass House on Ray, the gate had an old iron bell-pull, and Ken gave it a sharp tug. It must have sounded somewhere, because a young woman in a simplified version of a nun's habit came quickly to the gate.

'Can I help you?' Her accent couldn't have been more Irish if it had tried. Ken had always thought of the Irish as drunks, rough police or nuns, though what kind of a country could only produce those three professions was a mystery to him.

'We're here to see . . .' he began.

'. . . my mother,' Coraline completed. This was her family story, not his. 'Florence Tooke.'

The young nun looked at her blankly. 'There's no one here by that name,' she said, shaking her head.

Ken saw a flush of something in Coraline's cheek. 'I know she's here. Take me to her or it will be the police you'll be taking to her.'

The nun blinked nervously. 'I promise you, there is no one here with that name. If you want to fetch an officer, you may and—'

'If you make me, I will.'

'It won't make any difference. Upon my word.'

161

Ken put his hand on Coraline's shoulder. There was something in the young woman's expression that made him believe her. The journey they had made through dusty records and over freezing water and muddy tracks, it was all to end here at an iron fence in London. Disappointment was a bitter and rough pill.

'What?' Coraline demanded of him.

'I think she's telling the truth.'

'Then where the hell is she?' All the while, the nun was watching them with confusion visible on her face.

'I don't know. Let's leave. Let's—' He broke off as something clicked in his mind. The nun's precise words: *There's no one here by that name.* And what they implied. 'She's supposed to be dead. Of course they registered her under another name!'

'I'm sorry?' the nun replied, taken aback.

'She's here. Somewhere in your convent, there's a woman aged around fifty who's been here since 1920.'

'We . . . We have many patients who have been here that long.' She sounded more nervous now that these people might not just be lunatics.

'But there's something unique about this woman,' he said. 'This woman speaks with an American accent.' The nun's eyes widened and she glanced quickly over her shoulder at the buildings behind. 'I'm right, aren't I?'

The young woman hesitated, then nodded and relented. 'She's your mother?' she asked Coraline.

'Yes, she is. I want to see her.' Coraline was remaining cool, though Ken had the feeling that the young woman behind the gate shouldn't string this out too long.

'I only know her as Jessica. But . . .' She trailed off.

'No buts.' Coraline put her face close to the black iron. 'I'm not going to ask you again.'

Well, threatening a nun took the prize, but there was little else to do.

'I . . . need to speak to the Mother Superior.'

'You need to unlock this gate.'

Ken intervened. 'Go and ask her,' he said, calming the choppy waters. 'I suspect she knows Mrs Tooke's real name. Please tell her that Mrs Tooke's daughter is here. I presume any close family have the right to see their loved ones?'

'Well, y-yes,' the nun stammered. Then she swallowed hard and scurried towards the building.

'I want to kill my father,' Coraline said under her breath. 'How dare he do this?'

'Let's not jump to conclusions,' Ken cautioned. He had a feeling that things might not be as black and white as they seemed. And while passions were running high, it would be better to keep an even head.

She smoked two cigarettes from tip to tip as they waited for a response.

Eventually, the young nun returned, but she wasn't alone. A thick-set woman with a large wimple framing her face was striding towards them.

'Good afternoon,' she said, though her tone said it was a bad one.

'Good afternoon,' Ken replied, before Coraline could unleash the harsher language he guessed was on her mind. 'We're here to see Florence Tooke, or "Jessica", as you call her. This is her daughter, Coraline.'

'And you are?'

'A family friend. Ken Kourian.'

'A lawyer? Doctor?'

'Neither.'

'Then why would I concern myself with you?' She didn't wait for an answer, but spoke to Coraline. 'We will not allow you to speak to any of our patients. For one thing, I have no proof that you are even who you say you are.'

Coraline almost tore her purse apart opening it. She pulled out her crumpled packet of Nat Shermans and tossed it aside to rest in spiky weeds at the foot of the gate, before she found her cheque book. The younger nun bent down and discreetly picked up the cigarette packet. Coraline held out the pad of bank drafts. 'My name's right there,' she said, presenting one.

The elder nun took it from her through the bars and examined it, as if she might be able to detect some signs of forgery, before handing it back with a gesture that said it was unclean. 'You have shown me a banker's book. American. I cannot begin to say if it is yours.'

'What about your passport?' Ken suggested.

'It's in my valise, back at the Rose.'

'Well then,' the nun said. 'If you are who you claim to be, you will be quite able to write to the convent hospital and we will respond in the same way to the registered correspondence address. That is, if the woman you claim is our patient is indeed here.'

'You know damn well she is,' Ken muttered.

'Then you will have no trouble, will you?' she replied with a faint smirk. 'Come away, Sister Julia.' Sister Julia, who was holding on to the gate, followed the older woman. But as she turned to leave, she dropped something from the hand that was grasping the wrought iron. It was the cigarette packet.

'Damn them,' Coraline said under her breath. 'They don't care.'

'No,' Ken replied, distracted by the paper packet.

'My mother could die in there and I would be kept outside.'

His sight was still on the pack of Nat Shermans. 'Hold on, look.'

'At what?'

He stooped and reached through the twisting metal bars to the packet. It was rich green and sported the brand name in gold cursive lettering. But something had been written underneath the logo in pencil: 'East gate. An hour.'

'I think our young friend has a softer conscience than her boss,' he said, showing it to Coraline.

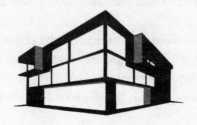

Chapter 15

'Do you remember anything about your mother?' Ken asked as they waited outside a thick door in the east wall.

'I remember her being kind.' Coraline paused. 'Not a specific act, more something around her. I suppose that's being a mother.' She gazed at a pine tree, glowing green in the hot noon light.

'Yes, I guess so.'

They waited until a metal noise alerted them to movement on the other side of the gate. A heavy bolt was being drawn back. The gate eased open and Sister Julia looked out cautiously. When she saw they were alone, she stood back without a word.

They followed her quickly and gratefully through the grounds, keeping to the bushes and trees at the edge, until they came to a rough-looking building connected to the main house by a covered walkway. Deep sounds drifted from it. The nun took a bunch of keys from her habit and let them into a whitewashed passage where the sounds solidified into a brew of humming and chanting.

'It's time for afternoon prayers,' the young woman whispered by way of explanation.

'Who's praying?' Ken asked, although he already knew.

'The patients. They're asking God for mercy.'

Something flared behind Coraline's eyes. 'Where's my mother?' she demanded.

The nun led them around a corner, past doors with heavy locks and numbers screwed to the wood. All were washed with thin white paint. The sister stopped at number five. A whispering from within, fast and low, as if the speaker had something urgent to tell but no time to do it, reached them and the young nun listened for a moment before she pushed in the key.

As she was about to turn it, she paused. 'Please, bear in mind that she's been here a long time. She's different to how you remember her.' The chain of electric lights above them buzzed.

'I was six when I was told she was dead.'

The nun attempted to say something, but the amazement had struck her dumb. She gave up and knocked on the door. 'Jessica,' she said. Then, hesitatingly, 'Florence?' The whispering stopped. The air hung cool despite the heat outside. 'Florence, I've got someone here to see you.

Visitors.' There was another burst of whispering, even faster than before.

The key turned and the door swung open on its own weight. They were looking into a small room like a religious cell. From a single window high up, nearly touching the ceiling, a beam of amber light was filtering in. Dust motes hung as it blazed onto a wall covered with images of the crucified Christ, his side pierced, his head torn by a crown of thorns. The Saviour's face, the colour of ash, spoke of the suffering of the man weighed down by all the sins of the world. And of the pain of the woman who had covered the walls with his image.

That woman was kneeling on the concrete floor, facing a wooden crucifix nailed to the wall below the window. The light made her yellow dress burn like the sun. In her right hand was a rosary, trailing on the floor. All they could see of her was her bent-over back.

'Jess ... Florence?' the sister asked. The whispering began again, slowly now, as her fingers touched the beads in sequence.

'*The fourth sorrowful mystery. The carrying of the cross.*' The sounds bounced around the room. Even the walls didn't want them.

'Florence, we're here.'

'*. . . full of grace. The Lord is with . . .*'

'Mama.' The name fell like a stone into water.

They all waited. The woman kneeling on the floor stiffened. The hand clutching the rosary withdrew towards her chest. 'Who is that?' Her accent was from New York.

'Me, Mama.'

The back unfurled and a woman's head lifted. Her hair had been a deep chestnut colour once, Ken thought, but now it was grey.

'Coraline.' Her voice no longer whispered. It spoke, low and watchful.

'Yes.' She stepped forward.

As she did so, her mother turned her head. The face of Florence Tooke, once delicate and rich with the ease of a wealthy life, had added flesh and lines and age and cares. But for sure it was the same one that had looked out from the newspapers. And the eyes, which were dark, crawled along the walls towards the three people behind her, across the young nun without interest, over Ken and to her youngest child.

'Coraline,' she said again. And it was said with satisfaction, as if she had been waiting a lifetime to mouth the syllables.

The faces of Jesus stared out at them all, faces dead and alive. Florence lifted the rosary, kissed it and hung it around her neck, all the while keeping her gaze on the three intruders into her devotions.

Finally, she turned her body to face them. The light surrounded her with a haze like embers from a wildfire. As she opened her arms, the blaze poured to the ground. 'I prayed to Him you would come,' she said. Coraline stepped forward, unafraid. 'Will you kiss me?'

Coraline could only take her mother's hands. But there was a question that couldn't wait even for the time it took to do that. 'Why are you here?' she asked.

Florence smiled, as if it was the only reply she had expected. 'Yes. Yes, why?'

'Did Father place you here?'

Florence turned back to face the cross on the wall. 'In a sense.' Among the images of Jesus of Nazareth, Ken saw, there was one other picture. It was a copy of a family portrait. He had seen it twice before: once hanging on a wall in the family home and once in grainy newsprint.

'In what sense? Did he force you here?'

The older woman smoothed down her hair. It was perfectly dressed and coiffed, as if she had taken great pains over it. 'Force me?'

Sister Julia interceded. 'I don't think you understand.'

'What do you mean?'

'Your mother's not detained here. She's here voluntarily. All the patients are.'

Florence moved to a bed in the corner of the room and, as she trod, Ken heard a strange noise: a mechanical clanking that he couldn't identify. She sat on the bed, neat and still, as if patience was something she had learned over the years. 'I've thought of you, all the time,' she said, dreamily. 'I asked Alexander about you.'

Her kidnapped son. So she was talking to the dead. That was not a healthy sign.

'You speak to Alexander?' Coraline prompted gently.

Florence turned to gaze at the family portrait on the wall. There they all were: the Governor, her, their three children. But beyond the oils on canvas, two of those figures were dead and one shut away.

'He came to see me.'

'When was that?'

'When?' Her mind became airy. 'Oh, last week. Last year. Time seems to flitter away in this place.'

Yes, not having a wristwatch or a calendar would do that. Ken glanced at the nun, but she didn't have an answer.

Coraline sat on the bed beside her mother. 'Alex died, Mama. More than twenty years ago.'

That revelation would be only one of two cuts, Ken knew. They would keep her other son's death from her for a while; dropping it on her now could have severe consequences. 'Is there a doctor we can speak to about her?' he asked the nun under his breath.

'Not now. He'll be here tomorrow.'

'What are you saying?' Florence asked her daughter.

'Alex died. When he was four.'

Florence sat back on the bed and smiled thinly. 'No, darling. He came to me last month. We spoke. I hadn't seen him for a long time.'

'Mama, he's not here anymore.'

'Why do you say that?' The cheer was fading from her lips.

'I'm sorry, it's the truth.'

'He sat right where you sit now.'

There was a hesitation. 'I don't think so.'

'I know he did.'

'Mama, how did you know it was him?'

'How did I know it was Alexander?'

'Yes.'

'A mother knows her own child,' she replied with quiet confidence.

At this, something occurred to Ken. It could just be that she had known her child, but the wrong one. 'Mrs Tooke,' he said. 'Could it have been Oliver, your other son, who came to see you? Is that possible?'

She gazed up at him. 'Oh, no, no. Not Oliver. It was Alexander. For sure.'

'No, Mama.'

'Is she on any kind of medication?' Ken asked the nun.

Florence relaxed, proud of herself. 'They gave me pills for a while. But I found it hard to think.'

'She stopped taking them,' Sister Julia said. 'We thought it safer not to force them on her.'

'Safer!' Florence laughed. 'For you.'

The news reports Ken had read described a society hostess who liked to paint watercolours. Had she ever been that statue of softness or had she, from the beginning, had a dark flame within her? And her insistence that her dead son had come to visit her could, depending on your point of view, have been an expression of deep-set religious faith or equally deep-set mania.

'The doctors want to help you.'

'No more doctors,' the distracted woman threatened. 'They put me here. They're behind it all. Plotting.' She strode furiously to the opposite corner of the room. The faint clinking sound went with her.

'It's a common delusion,' the nun said as quietly as she could.

'What do you know about it, girl?' Florence snapped, with a filthy look. 'What do any of you know?'

'Your doctor—'

172

Florence interrupted. 'Yes, the doctor. Ask him. He's behind it all. He was in on it with my husband.'

'Which doctor?' Ken asked.

She became angrier. 'That one. With the broken mouth. I told Alexander about him. The injection.'

Ken addressed Sister Julia. 'Do you know who she means?'

She shook her head. 'Are you a little confused, Florence?'

Coraline's mother ignored the question. There was that queer metal noise again as she shifted her weight, like someone was tapping a tin can. 'What's that sound?' Ken asked the nun.

But it was Florence who replied. 'That's my sin,' she whispered. 'A remembrance of my guilt.'

'What?'

In answer, Florence reached down, pinched the material of her dress and began to pull it up, her eyes locked to his.

'Mama.'

'Hush, child.' And the cotton slipped up her flesh, exposing a bare calf, then the pink of her thigh. 'Here, you see my guilt.' The dress rose higher still. The nun let her head drop, as if she knew what was coming and didn't want to admit it. And then the hem lifted over a ring of chain metal studded with sharp barbs. All of them were turned inwards, spiking into angry flesh and piercing the skin to draw pin-pricks of blood. 'I mortify my flesh to atone for what I have done.' She gazed happily upon the item. 'And through my remembrance of sin, I shall sit at the table of the Lord.' Her gaze lifted to the other three in the room, one by one. 'You too shall atone for your sins.'

'What the hell is *that*?' Ken demanded of Sister Julia. He was angry and amazed in equal measures, but the anger won out.

'A cilice. She's right, religiously speaking. But . . .'

'But what?'

'We don't use them for the patients. They're for members of the order.' She touched her own thigh and Ken understood. 'She begged us for one. Eventually, the Mother Superior said that if she wanted to live like a member of our order, there was no shame in that. She got what she wanted.'

Florence touched her rosary to her lips again and began to chant to herself. '*The first sorrowful mystery . . .*' The fire in her withdrew and she turned in on herself.

'Sometimes it's what you want that's going to kill you,' Coraline said, watching her mother. 'So if she's not detained here, she can leave? Right now, if she wants.'

The nun looked like she regretted speaking up. Maybe she should have guessed what would be just about the first thing on a daughter's mind. 'Well, yes, but I'm not sure that's a—'

Coraline was taking no interruptions. 'Mama, would you like to leave here?'

'Please can we speak in the corridor?' the nun asked urgently.

They withdrew, leaving Ken alone with Florence. She smiled at him, and he couldn't miss a hint of something spreading along her lips; a hint of long-forgotten coquetry, like perfume in the air after a party has ended. It wasn't nice to see.

174

'What's your name?'

'Ken,' he told her. 'Ken Kourian.'

'Are you going to take me away, Ken?' she said, her voice breathy. 'Just you and me?' She stood in the orange beam of afternoon sun. He wondered if this had once been part of her life, her character. The newspapers would never have reported it because the upper classes always closed ranks against that kind of scandal. She came closer. 'Will it be just you and me?' He looked up at the family portrait. She saw where his gaze had fixed. 'That's all gone.'

She came closer again and he raised a hand to press her away from him. 'I don't think that's a good idea,' he said.

'It will be good for both of us.'

'No.'

'And why not?' She pushed out her lower lip in a bad actress's gesture of petulance.

'You're safe here.'

There was a pause, then she spoke again. 'Ken says he's going to take me away. Just me and him.'

He guessed what had happened. Over his shoulder, he saw Coraline and the nun had re-entered the room.

'What did you say to her?' the sister demanded, not bothering to hide the accusation.

'Nothing,' he replied. There was no point trying to explain and it would have seemed in poor taste. Florence sat on the bed but her smile stayed.

'Outside,' Coraline said. She, the nun and Ken withdrew into the corridor to confer. 'I want to take her home,' Coraline declared.

GARETH RUBIN

'But it will be a dreadful shock to her,' replied the nun. 'It's hard to say how she will cope.'

'That will be up to us.'

'You need to speak to the Mother Superior.'

Coraline paused for a second. 'I want to know who the doctor is, the one she was speaking about.'

'I have no idea. I'm sorry.'

They heard Florence begin to whisper, fast and low, once more.

'We can try to find him,' Ken said. 'But are you certain you want to take her away? Now?'

'If I wait, and my father discovers we were here, he might prevent it. He might move her somewhere we'll never find her.'

Ken wasn't so sure. He didn't know the right shot and didn't want to do anything that would seem crazy in retrospect. 'We don't know yet why he did this.'

'Whatever the reason,' she said, fixing him with her gaze, 'she's better off not spending her days surrounded by those pictures. If she wasn't out of her mind before she went in, that would be enough to do it. She's coming with us.'

But before he could answer, there was a new voice. It shook the bricks in their mortar. 'That is not your decision to make!' The Mother Superior was coming towards them at speed. There was someone behind her in the narrow corridor, keeping pace.

'Then whose is it?' Coraline demanded.

And the man behind the Mother Superior, a man Ken had met twice on the other side of the Atlantic Ocean, spoke with cold fury as he strode past the nun towards them. 'It is mine,' he snarled. 'You take her out of here and she'll cut her wrists. Or hang herself. Or wade into the sea, and this time she'll succeed.'

'You lied to me for twenty years,' Coraline spat.

Governor Tooke was ten paces away and closing fast. 'I kept you from a truth that would have caused you more pain than you could ever know.' The senior nun, who must have summoned him from somewhere nearby, looked every bit as angry as he did. 'Unlike you, I've had to live with it.' He glared a thousand daggers at Ken. 'My son brought you to my home. Now I find you digging into my family affairs. Get the hell out of here before I have you arrested.'

Ken was about to tell him where to go when Coraline did it for him. 'He's with me, Father. And you have no more jurisdiction here than a farmhand.'

'Please,' begged Sister Julia, trying to get between them. 'Please calm down. This will be upsetting for your mother and for our other patients.'

'That's enough from you!' the Mother Superior growled.

The Governor glanced darkly at his daughter and Ken, then strode into his wife's room and closed the door with a bang. Florence's whispering ceased immediately.

'Hello, my dear,' they heard the Governor say. 'I'm afraid I have some very bad news.' And he told her something too quiet for them to hear, and there was silence before the sound of a woman's voice screaming. Coraline opened the door but her father filled the frame and pushed her away, slamming it shut.

The air in the corridor was stale as they waited, simmering in what they had done. The younger nun took a few steps away, discreetly distancing herself from them. Ken didn't blame her. She had done her best to do the right thing, and now it would rebound on her. The Mother Superior glared at them in succession.

'I want a drink,' Coraline said.

'You and me both.'

For the next few minutes, they heard muffled voices and made out the occasional word: 'Oliver', 'funeral'. And then more silence.

Eventually, the Governor emerged, his face dark as coal. 'Follow me,' he ordered them.

Coraline ignored his instruction and brushed past him into her mother's room. Florence was sitting on the bed, staring up at the carved image of Christ on the cross, beads of wooden blood on his forehead. She didn't seem to realize that her daughter was there at all. The life had ebbed from her, as if the news of Oliver's death had drained away the little she had left.

Coraline sat on the bed too and put her arms around her mother's shoulders. She hadn't done so since she was six, Ken knew. It had to be like hugging a stranger to her. And yet she did it and her cheek found her mother's.

'You want to know why I convinced her to come here,' Governor Tooke said, straightening his tie. They were walking in the grounds of the convent. The scent of the honeysuckle hung heavy on the air. His anger was subsiding into weariness.

'Make it a damn good story, Father,' Coraline cautioned.

'Oh, I have no need to embellish things, girl.' He sat on a felled tree and stretched out his neck. 'You've always thought yourself clever. Well, we shall see. We shall see.' He paused, as if remembering a time that he had long suppressed in his memory. 'When Alexander was abducted, your mother told the police that two gypsy men had taken him from her in the garden at Turnglass and run off to the mainland.'

'I know,' she replied. 'I know it all.'

'So you think.'

'What are you getting at?'

He ignored her question. 'But have you thought about it? What, they just walked up to the house without any of us or the staff seeing them, and waltzed right out again while your mother screamed blue murder?' Coraline's face clouded a little with thought, the change seeming to suggest she understood his drift. 'Oh, yes, I see. You're beginning to think. Not so clever now, are you? And tell me this: why did they do it?' He threw his hands up. 'A thrill kill, they said. Well, they were always talking about those, even back then. Thrill kill.' He shook his head angrily. 'Utter garbage. You get the odd nutjob, for sure, but for the most part they take a hatchet to their own mothers, they don't plan the kidnap of a wealthy man's little boy. And they don't work in pairs. And they don't go all the way out to Ray to do it.' The weariness enveloped him entirely. 'No, I don't believe that pat little explanation dreamed up by cops who had no clue and a bunch of trash newspapermen who wanted to sell more copies of their bilge. Pity, in a way, because it would be easier for everyone if it was some crazy stranger we never had to think about again.' He picked over his own words. 'I've hoped, of course. Hoped that one of those gypsies would get drunk and confess or get picked up for some other crime, then I could tie the rope myself. But I don't think that's going to happen. No, sir.' He took off his jacket in the heat, folded it neatly beside him on the trunk and sat staring at it.

'I presumed it was a kidnapping for money,' Coraline suggested.

'Then where was the ransom demand?' His exasperation burst out like he had been bottling it for twenty-five years. 'We waited weeks for one. If you take someone for money, you ask for it. Even if something had gone wrong and Alexander had died, they would still have sent a demand, a piece of his clothing, and we would have paid up in the hope of getting him back. But there wasn't anything. So what could the motive have possibly been?'

Coraline said nothing for a while. Then she knitted her fingers together and spoke. 'You think Mama had something to do with it,' she said, her voice betraying a fear that hadn't been there before.

'Honestly, I don't know,' he sighed. Ken had to feel sorry for the man, hectoring though he had been until then. 'She had been . . . unstable for some time. And then that happened and the police could find no trace.'

'Whatever made you think you could get away with hiding her like this?'

He lifted his eyes and thought for a moment before

answering. 'Your grandfather taught me that a man does what he knows is right. Even if all other men tell him it's wrong. I've lived by that. All my life.'

Ken looked at the Governor, a man who had had his two sons taken from him. Who could come back from that kind of trauma without scars? Not many.

'She said that Alex visited her,' Coraline said.

'Good God,' Tooke muttered. 'The things she believes. She used to be better – in some ways.'

'What do you mean?'

He took a handkerchief from his top pocket and dabbed his neck. 'When she was taking her medication. She was … slow in her thoughts. But the ideas weren't outlandish. She's gotten worse. The doctors tell me that's not unusual.'

They sat for a while, listening to the garden birds and gazing towards the block where a number of small barred rooms contained women.

'She wants to go home, Father. It's time. It could help. The scandal's over. If she has round-the-clock supervision, she'll be safe. She might even come back to us.'

'She won't.'

'She might.'

He hesitated. 'How could I even get her home?'

'You haven't broken any law, not back home anyway. And you can make it discreet.'

'She doesn't even have a passport.'

'Then go to the embassy and get one. All the officials will know is that an American woman, the wife of the Governor of California, needs a new passport. They won't do any checking, and even if they do they're not going to rock the boat. You're a powerful man. You can be on an airplane in forty-eight hours. Do it, Father.'

'And then what?'

'Then what? A private nursing home. Somewhere quiet.'

'Nowhere's that discreet.'

'Somewhere must be. And we can cross the next bridge when we come to it. If you don't, I'll do it myself. And that will make a lot more noise.'

Tooke dabbed his neck again. 'All right. All right. I guess it's time.'

'I think your father cares about your mother. And about Oliver too,' Ken said. They were in the lobby of the Savoy Hotel on the Strand. The Governor, who had already taken a suite, had told them to take rooms there while he remained at the convent to arrange his wife's discharge. They could return to Mersea for their baggage when it was all in hand. A commissionaire in green velvet and sparkling war medals had touched his fingers to his top hat as they had entered and Ken had finally got his taste of old-manners London, though he hadn't been in the mood to enjoy it.

'You know what he used to say?' Coraline replied. '"A strong house is built over generations." He told Oliver that he would be the one to follow in Father's footsteps and complete what our grandfather had begun – our family's rise to the very top. That's why Father gave Oliver his name.'

The receptionist was filling out a form for their stay. 'It's not unusual,' Ken replied. 'Many men want their sons to be like them.'

'Father wants to be President. If he can't be, he wanted Oliver to be. Now what does he have? The Tookes will die out with him.'

Ken actually felt a slim stroke of sympathy for the Governor, a man who put his family name above everything else. He felt more sympathy for the man's wife, though, whose mind had been broken by her loss. 'It was Oliver who went to see her,' he said. 'She thought he was Alex.'

'I know.'

And that told them something. 'Coraline,' he said, shifting so he could look her in the eye. 'I don't think it's a coincidence that your brother discovers your mother's alive and then dies.'

She licked her lips. 'No.'

There was a long pause. A guest was complaining about the sound of airplanes over London. The concierge was explaining the possibility of war. It was being dismissed as a phony excuse for the noise. 'You ever think about your grandfather and that house on Ray?' Ken said.

'What about them?'

He smoothed his hand over his scalp. 'There's something I can't shake from my head.'

'What do you mean?'

'It's a sense that everything that's happened – to you, your brother, us – is a set of dominoes. The first fell in 1881; the next in 1915; then 1920. Now we're dealing with the last of them.'

'You realize that sounds crazy.'

'Sure it does. But I also think it's true.'

The receptionist arranged for their small bags to be sent up to their rooms and they went to the American Bar to drink martinis. The barman slid them down the zinc bar.

'I'll be square with you,' Ken said, after they had emptied three glasses each in silence. 'I've dreamed of coming to London for most of my life.'

'And what do you think?'

'Well, this isn't what I thought it would be.' He watched a troop of soldiers hurry past the window. Britain was more frantic than he had ever pictured it. It was buzzing with a mix of defiance and fear of the future. The country had been through a bad war twenty years earlier and it wasn't looking forward to another.

'What did you think it would be?'

He stared at the troops and the traffic honking like hopped-up geese. 'Quieter.'

They drank. And hours later, after the electric lights had been turned on, they were sent word that Governor Tooke had returned and required their presence. They drained their glasses and made their way to the elevator. Ken could tell that the alcohol and time to brood had given a bump to the anger Coraline had suppressed at the convent. There was a flinty look in her eyes that turned to hard rock as they rose up the floors.

A hotel page took them to the crown suite, which had been decked out for a king with better taste than most of them actually had. The Governor was talking on the telephone. He was speaking loudly and slowly, and Ken guessed the call was travelling along wires sitting on the Atlantic seabed.

'. . . of course you can. Be my guest.' A pause. 'Oh, nothing to speak of. Only that my secretary had a call from an old friend of his at the *Globe* asking if he knew anything about an automobile accident in Florida.' He paused briefly, and his tone changed, becoming more confidential. 'I don't like that kind of politics, Sam. But if you're going to come up against me . . .' He paused again, this time waiting for a reply, and Ken heard a light creaking through the earpiece, although he couldn't make out the words. 'No, no, of course you aren't. Well, that's fine news. And I'll instruct my secretary to assure his friend that the girl is lying – she had a couple of bruises, no more, it's all exaggerated, not worth the reporter's time. Yes, agreed. November it is. It's been a pleasure speaking to you, Sam, as it always is. And give my regards to Beatrice.' He hung up, stood, thoughtful for a while, then sat in a wing-backed leather chair and waited for Coraline to speak. It was clear that the atmosphere was different to when the three of them had sat in the convent garden and Tooke had seemed apologetic, almost ashamed over what he had done.

It was a while before Coraline spoke. The question was heavy. 'Father, how could you bring yourself to do it?'

He poured bourbon for all three of them.

'I had my family to think of,' he told the bottle.

'She *is* your family.'

'Not all of it. I have ancestors, and one day I expect to have descendants. I have a duty to them too.'

'Duty?' The bourbon remained undrunk.

'Yes, my girl. Duty. You spit out that word like it's dirty. It isn't.'

'Are you going to tell me about being President again?'

He seemed irked but kept his voice level. 'Yes, that will be a duty to our country.'

Coraline slowly drew on a pair of blue kid gloves. It was to give her time to think, Ken could tell. 'Let's just talk about Mother and the arrangements for taking her home.'

Half an hour later, Ken dropped onto his soft bed and ran through all that he knew and didn't know. There was more on the second list. Oliver had been killed, of that he was certain. His death was most likely linked to his mother's incarceration in the asylum where she had taken on a religious bent, obsessed with her own guilt; but why would that push someone to kill Oliver? What if . . .

Something caught his eye.

The handle on his bolted door was moving down and there was the sound of a creaking floorboard outside. He watched the handle move. It could be whoever had been asking questions about them at the Peldon Rose. Or it could be her. The time on the airplane that they had nearly kissed had been playing on the inside of his skull like an orchestra.

The handle changed direction, lifting again, returning to its proper position. He waited. There was a light sound, breathing. And a very slight tapping of feet on the floor.

And then he heard whoever it was try the handle of the next room along: Coraline's.

He jumped up, barefoot, shirtless, and unbolted and flung open the door. No one to be seen, but he hadn't imagined it. He rapped on her door. Nothing. No sound of stirring. He looked down the staircase and tried again, more forcefully.

'Coraline,' he said.

At that he heard movement, the sound of clothes being slipped on or off. The door opened to him on a brass chain. Her eyes appeared above it. He knew they were milky blue, but in that light they were darker than coal.

He was going to explain that someone had tried to enter his room – hers too – and that it could be nothing or something, but then he didn't, he just waited for her to speak.

She didn't. She unhooked the chain and let it fall.

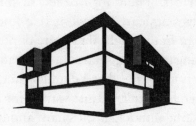

Chapter 16

They stayed in London for two days, then returned to Mersea to collect their bags, before flying back over the Atlantic and then to Sacramento, where they caught a late train to Los Angeles. The lights of lonely small towns flashed past the blind, creating a flicker-book of shapes and shadows. They became less frequent, more remote, until they disappeared completely as the wilderness of the American west took over. Few houses or farms out here. California was a state of cities. The movies were there for the daylight; the actors were there for the fame; Simeon Tooke had arrived half a century ago for the optimism. Everyone was looking to the future in California.

They pulled into Central Station, six days after they left Mersea, as the sun was setting. 'Shall we talk to Carmen now?' Coraline asked.

They knew why she had lied at the inquest about seeing Florence drown, but Ken wanted to know what she had said to Oliver on the day Ken had first met Coraline. Whatever it was had upset them both.

He looked at his wristwatch. 'It's late. We'll talk tomorrow.'

They said goodnight and he took a streetcar back to his lodging house. He managed to spend a night in his own bed for the first time in weeks.

He slept like a log and when he woke he didn't even need a coffee to speed him on his way to the Tooke house.

Coraline was waiting for him in the library, which carried the same lugubrious air as before, as if it was expecting bad news. Carmen was sent for, and entered looking uncomfortable. News of the secrets surfacing within the family must have reached the servants.

'My mother is alive,' Coraline said after a mile-long silence. Carmen bit her lip and stared at her hands. 'Did you know that?' Tears welled in the old woman's eyes and she nodded quickly. 'You've always known.'

'Governor Tooke told me and no one else,' she whispered. 'Sometimes I had to send her things. Clothes or little keepsakes.' She looked up blearily. 'I just wanted to look after her, miss. I've looked after you all.'

Coraline went to the windows that led out to the garden, leaving the maid staring at her back.

189

Ken took up the conversation. 'Oliver found out, didn't he?' She nodded again. 'He said that to you.'

'Yes, sir.'

'Did he say anything else?'

'He asked for old photographs of the family. *All* the family.' She said it with meaning. She didn't want to name Alexander, the missing child. His name was black magic in this house, that was becoming clear.

'And that's it?'

'Yes, sir. Only that and asking about himself when he was young. What I remember about him. Whether he was a happy boy; if he was unhappy in his wheelchair.'

'And what did you say?'

'I only came to the family after Alex's ...' She shot a nervous glance at Coraline's back. '... disappearance. So I didn't know him younger. But no boy's happy in a wheelchair.'

They dismissed her. Ken felt sorry for the woman, who had been forced into a conspiracy she neither understood nor gained from.

He drummed his fingers on a bookcase. 'Your mother said something about a doctor. "He's behind it all. He was in on it with my husband." That's what she said.' He started to ponder. It was following in Simeon's footsteps in *The Turnglass* that had led him to Florence. Oliver had been leaving breadcrumbs through the forest. So where else had Simeon gone? 'A doctor with ...' He trailed off, as he remembered something. '... with a broken mouth,' he continued, more to himself than to Coraline. 'Let me see your copy of Oliver's book.' She went to her room and returned with the novel. Ken searched for a passage: Simeon in the smog-addled Limehouse docks.

> Simeon's vision fell on a man on a bunk. Unlike the others, the man was not smoking his opium, but sipping from a green bottle. He had a hare lip, which was causing the liquid to dribble down his chin.

'Here!' Ken cried out. He read out the lines.

> 'Would you like to try a little, sir?' the man asked. He grinned, to show a maw devoid of teeth. Yet his voice was educated. A university man, by the sound of it. 'The lower-life people in this establishment like to chase the dragon. Me, I prefer to drown it in brandy.'
>
> 'So I see,' Simeon replied. 'But laudanum is just as addictive, you must understand.'
>
> 'Oh, oh, you need not tell me, sir. I am a full fellow of the Royal College of Surgeons.'

'Don't you recall someone who fits that description?' Ken asked.

'Should I?'

'A doctor with a hare lip.' Her face remained blank. 'That doctor your father brought here to bully Senator Burrows just before your brother was killed. He had a hare lip. It's too much to be a coincidence. Oliver included him in the story because he played a part in what happened – and your mother said the doctor behind what had happened to her had a broken mouth; and something about injections too.'

She nodded in agreement. 'His name was Kruger, the one Father brought here.'

'Well, we can see if we can track him down. And I've just realized something else.'

'What's that?'

'All this is coming from the book. But authors write many drafts of their books.'

'So . . .'

'So what if Oliver wrote an earlier version?' He was excited, warming to the idea. 'A draft he cut down to fit into the right number of pages or something. There could be more details to help us.'

'It's possible.'

'Yeah. But first, we'll try to find Dr Kruger.'

A call to the state medical board confirmed that a man with that name did indeed hold a licence to practise, and of course they could supply his surgery address and number. Ken slapped the wall in triumph.

'Dr Kruger's surgery.' It was a pleasant and matronly southern voice hissing through the line.

'I would like an appointment,' Ken informed her.

'Certainly, sir. May I take your name?'

He gave a false one. 'How soon could he see me?'

'I can offer you an appointment tomorrow at two. Is that good?'

'I was hoping to see him before that.'

'I'm sorry, but he's busy until then.'

'I see. Okay, book me in.' He gave her a false address, she made the appointment and he ended the call.

'Do you think anything will come of it?' Coraline asked.

'Maybe, maybe not. Now I want to see if we can find any other versions of the book.'

According to the title page of Coraline's copy, it was Daques Publishing that they had to contact; and their offices were in LA, so Ken and Coraline drove over. It turned out to be a young company not shy about its ambitions, judging by the size of the office. After conversations with the receptionist, and then the head receptionist, in which they explained what they had come for, they were eventually admitted to a conference room with shining silver leather armchairs around a long table and shelves lined with books. On the other side of the table, with a sheaf of papers in front of him that he was scoring with a red pen, a man with a sardonic glint in his spectacles listened to their plea. This was Oliver's editor, they were told, Sid Cohen.

'Mr Kourian, Miss Tooke, I'm in something of a quandary,' said Cohen, sitting back and making a pyramid of his fingers. 'You see, believe it or not, you aren't the first people to come here saying almost exactly the same thing.'

'*What?*' Ken replied. It was a surprise and not a welcome one.

'In fact, I have to tell you, you're aren't even the first people in the last seventy-two hours saying almost exactly the same thing.'

Coraline looked daggers.

'What do you mean, sir?' Ken asked.

'I mean, a guy came here three days ago saying he represented the Tooke family, and politely but firmly requested I hand over any previous drafts of Oliver's latest book.'

'My family has authorized no such individual,' Coraline insisted bitterly. 'Who was he?'

Cohen tapped his pen ruminatively. 'My problem, miss, is that if there is some kind of subterfuge going on, who do I believe? Before the other man came, I got a letter announcing his visit on the headed notepaper of a well-known legal firm. Now, it could have been faked – pretty easily, really, I wasn't on my guard so I didn't exactly check up to see if they really had sent him – but also it could have been real. So here's my quandary: is he the genuine article or are you?'

'Want to see my driver's licence?' she shot back. Ken could tell that after the incident at the convent, she was getting pretty damn tired of having to prove her identity to people who had a very loose connection to her family.

'Yes, I think that would do it.'

Coraline opened the clasp on her clutch bag and drew out her purse. She took out her licence and a photograph and pushed them across the table. Cohen took up the licence, then the photo, peered at them and returned them respectfully. Ken caught sight of a snapshot in which Coraline and her brother were lit by flashbulbs, arm in arm at some party. 'I believe you. But I don't think it's going to help you much. I believed the other guy and gave him the previous drafts Oliver sent in.'

'What did this man look like?' Ken asked.

Cohen shrugged. 'It was a few days ago, so I don't remember all that well. But he looked, well . . . ordinary.'

'Ordinary?'

'Yes. But that's what stood out. He was so ordinary it was surreal.'

'Are there any more copies of those drafts?' Ken asked. He knew the man they were talking about.

'Sorry.'

'Do you remember anything from them? Any major changes?'

'I'll be honest with you. I work on ten books at once. I barely remember their titles, let alone changes to the text. So I'm sorry, but I can't help you there.' He sucked thoughtfully on the pen like a cigarette. 'Why do you want to know?'

'Doesn't matter now. Thanks for your time.'

They returned to the car. 'Brick wall,' Ken muttered angrily as he wrenched open the door.

'It seems so.'

'Damn it. Right, screw waiting until tomorrow. I'm pissed. We're going over to Kruger's surgery now.'

'If you say so.'

It was fifteen minutes' drive over to Dr Kruger's consulting rooms in a well-to-do street off Olympic, where it was hard to imagine anyone needing any medical attention unless it was for the effects of too rich a diet. They stopped outside.

'What are you going to say to him?' Coraline asked. She didn't take the trouble to hide her scepticism.

'I'll ask him if he's treated any members of your family.'

'He'll probably tell you where to go.'

'If he does, we haven't lost anything.'

As they spoke, a kindly-looking man wearing spectacles

and carrying a black medical bag emerged from the office. Ken recognized him and began to walk over, but the man raised his hand towards a cab and the car stopped. He jumped in and the taxi drove away.

'Get in,' Coraline said.

They followed the cab through light traffic, keeping their distance. It wasn't hard at that time of day. And when they came to a halt, it was outside an office building that had been completed so recently it probably didn't even have a vermin problem yet. A brass plaque screwed to the wall announced the presence of a medical association: 'American Eugenics Society'. Ken knew of a national body that campaigned to have physically or mentally ill 'defectives' removed from the population. He thought of Florence, how she had been shut away.

Kruger was hurrying up the steps. Ken jumped out and called to him. 'Dr Kruger!' Kruger stopped and looked round. When he came close, Ken saw again the hare lip that Oliver had noted. 'I don't know if you remember, but we met before very briefly.'

'Did we?'

'It was at Governor Tooke's house.'

Kruger's eyebrows lifted in mild interest, a little taken aback by the approach in the street. 'Oh?'

'He has asked me to speak to you about something.'

The eyebrows fell again, his expression narrowing in suspicion. 'Governor Tooke sent you to speak to me?'

'Yes.'

'Why?' He snapped the question; the genial glow had dimmed to nothing.

'About how you treated Mrs Tooke.' The doctor sized him up without speaking. 'My own wife suffers in the same way.'

'Does she?' It was guarded, giving nothing away.

'I might have to put her in an institution.'

'Then do so.' There was a finality to Kruger's tone as he said it. 'I am not the physician you need. So why don't you go back to Governor Tooke – if he did indeed send you – and ask again.' With that, he stomped towards the building entrance. A huge security guard leaning against the doorpost seemed to be taking a keen interest. He had an air about him of wanting to do something destructive with his fists.

'Dr Kruger.'

'I have nothing more to say.'

'Doctor, wait!'

Ken followed him. But the security guard stepped forward and pressed his beefy palm against Ken's chest. 'Back off, chum,' he warned. Ken threw the hand aside and pushed past.

'Kru—' The name was strangled, forced back into Ken's windpipe by a solid arm thrown around his throat from behind. Automatically, his hands grabbed for it, but it held tight and he could feel himself being toppled off his feet. He saw Kruger drop his medical bag in surprise.

Ken could feel the muscular arm was strong, but he wasn't in the mood for heroes. A sharp elbow into the man's gut broke the grasp. He whirled around and launched a fist into the guard's sternum, winding him.

Then it was Greco-Roman wrestling all the way and Ken was motivated as hell.

'You two stop that!' The voice was accustomed to barking orders, and in a second a police officer had come between them. 'What the heck's going on here?'

Kruger came back down from the building entrance. 'That man was harassing me,' he said, pointing a stick-like finger at Ken.

'That so? How?'

'Asking me questions.'

'You know him?'

'Not at all. Keep him away from me.'

Ken could tell he wasn't going to get any answers from the doctor, but at least he could cause him some trouble. 'I just want to know what you did to Florence Tooke.' He rubbed his throat. He was getting tired of sustaining injuries on someone else's behalf. 'That's the wife of Governor Tooke,' he added for the benefit of the policeman. It was always worth throwing in a political connection if you wanted the police to actually take notice of you.

'I've never treated her,' Kruger declared.

'Oh really?' He strung it out like a fishing line. 'Then why did you just tell me you had?'

'I said no such thing.' Kruger was looking rattled. This was not what he had expected this morning.

'Sure you didn't.'

'I've had enough of this. Officer, that man was harassing me. Please get him away from me.'

'You want me to arrest him?'

'Yeah, let's make this official,' Ken said, holding out his wrists for cuffs.

Kruger's mouth opened but he hesitated, deciding if he did want to make this official.

The cop shifted his shoulder blades under his tunic. This was more trouble than he was looking for. He saw the deal and spoke to Ken. 'In that case, I want your name and address, then you're walking away.'

Ken told him, after which the officer marched him up the street with a firm hand on his shoulder, leaving no doubt that he would be better off taking a hike. Coraline raised a pencilled eyebrow at the escort when they got to her.

'That went well,' she said.

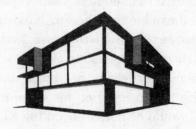

Chapter 17

Back at his apartment, nursing a bruised neck, Ken found a telephone message from his boss asking if he was ever going to come back or if they should just sack him now. He screwed it up and threw it aside. No, he wouldn't be going back.

He took a bath, listening to the radio. There was a play on about a man sick of the crime in his neighbourhood. He recruited his friends into a vigilante committee, only for corruption to seep in and the committee to become worse than the criminals they were trying to stop. It was followed by a news programme that reported more military build-up in Europe and a weather warning for the California coastline. A tropical storm was brewing at sea that could make landfall soon. Batten down your hatches, the newscaster said, it could be a bad one.

Ken spent a few hours thinking over what his next move should be. Florence was atoning for a sin that only she knew. But if it was to do with the abduction of Alexander Tooke, it would be best to know more of that crime than he had gleaned from a few newspaper articles.

He went to a phone box and called the Tooke house.

'Hello?' came the soft reply.

'It's me.' He felt determined.

A pause. 'I thought it would be.'

'I want to come over.'

'Come at seven.'

And then there was another voice in the background, a man asking, 'Where to, Miss Tooke?'

'The Yacht Club,' she replied, away from the mouthpiece. The family chauffeur was on duty. 'Ken?' she asked, returning to the conversation.

'Yeah.'

'What do you think happened in 1915? To Alex.'

'It looks like your mother was responsible. And Kruger's mixed up in her being hidden away after that. I guess your father arranged for it to happen in England because there were fewer people around who knew her. No one to intervene. Makes sense, when you think about it.'

It looks.

I guess.

When you think about it.

The only thing around here that was black and white was the floor of the Tookes' lobby.

'At seven,' she repeated. And she put the phone down, her voice replaced by an empty buzz on the line.

So murky, these waters. And it was no stretch to admit that he barely knew Coraline any more than he knew the rest of her family. What she felt, what she was thinking, was only what she wanted him to see.

That evening, as the hour hand on his wristwatch moved to the figure seven and the minute hand clicked onto the twelve, he dismissed a cab and approached the glass-sided house. The lights were off, leaving it to sparkle with reflected glimmers from the sea. It was the wrong house for the Tooke family. It was see-through, allowing everyone to look in, while the people who lived there did their best to hide their lives away.

He pulled the bell and it rang without an answer. She must have been out and running late, but it was a fine night, so he went around to the beach side to sit out on the sand until Coraline returned.

As he sauntered along the shoreline, bathing in the California heat after the European chill, he gazed at the writing tower, standing in the sea like the last debutante at a summer ball. Had anyone been there to lock it up or empty it of all Oliver's books? It would be like picking away at the carrion of a man's life. He glanced back at the house. It had only been a few months since couples had danced and trumpeters blown; now that might well never have happened. And something stood out: the back door wasn't completely shut.

He went closer. 'Coraline?' No answer. He eased

the door open. In the deep copper light, the glass had become a hall of tinted mirrors and the sheen of the sun reflected around the room to make a forest of red discs. Rippling blue sea appeared under each one, surrounding the room so that it was cut off from the land, like the other, older, house. For a moment, he felt an empathy with Oliver, closed in and trapped his whole life by glass.

The waves rolled behind him as he slipped in. But there was something else on top of their sound. Music. Violins – classical – were being played. Vivaldi, he thought. Someone, somewhere in the house, was listening to a record or the radio. He called Coraline's name again, but there was no reply.

He rounded the baby grand piano, went across the room and through to the hallway. He stopped to listen – the violins were stronger now, coming from the upper floor. The white marble staircase glowed faintly and the violins soared to a violent crescendo as he climbed. 'Coraline?' he called once more. The suspicion was growing on him that something was wrong.

His shoes tapped on the marble, a drum-beat below the violins. It was impossible to say where they were coming from. The red doorway led to what had been Oliver's room. It faced the setting sun and the light was bright, picking out the detritus of life: a bed; clothes still hanging in the closet; a set of binoculars on a hook by the window. No one there.

The next room was the green-doored library, there to remind any visitor that this was a venerable family; but a telephone and telex machine were ready in the corner to demonstrate wealth and modernity too.

That left a pair of guest bedrooms and Coraline's own room. The music grew heavier as Ken stalked along the corridor. He came to her door of blue smoked glass and to the source of the strings on the other side. He knocked. No answer. 'Coraline.' Nothing still. But then a new sound: a distant creaking. He took hold of the handle and opened the door a little. A blade of light pierced the gap towards him. 'Are you there?' The creaking again. He pushed the door open and the sea filled his vision: a bank of windows looking out across the ocean, a white leather sofa in front of them. The violins drew above the waves and the groaning wood; but something was breaking the wide expanse of the sea, something hanging from the ceiling. It twisted in the breeze from an open window: a bare foot, a slender form in a cotton dress and atop the shoulders a head hanging forward.

'Coraline!' He charged in, knocking over a side table, so that a collection of perfume bottles broke, spraying little pools of golden liquid across the floor.

The woman's form hung from a rope noose attached to a light fitting. Her back was to him, her head bowed over on a broken neck. He caught hold of her legs in a desperate hope that life might still be there. Below her, a soft leather shoe rested on the floor. But as Ken's hands gripped her calves, one look at the face above him told him a pair of bitter truths.

The first was that the life that had once burned brightly in this body had been snuffed out and could never come back, no matter how many prayers were said, no matter how skilful the doctors who attended. It was gone like the light of a previous day.

The second truth that forced itself upon him, stopping his breath in his chest, was that the woman he held, the woman turning in the breeze, wasn't the unknowable Coraline Tooke.

No. The poor woman he was holding up was her mother, Florence. Tragic, abused, remorseful Florence. She hung by a white industrial cord. It had been meant for rough timber or boats.

He let her go. The metal garter that bit into the flesh of her thigh, to pay penance for old sins, clinked with the movement. It had done her no good. God had not been on her side, had never been on the side of the family who lived in this house. This house that had seen two deaths.

And then a thought struck: *Let there be only two.*

He rushed along the corridor, bursting into both unexplored guest rooms and then the Governor's bedroom, checking them with a single glance, then down into the kitchen. But Coraline wasn't there. No one was. And when he returned to the bedroom and the hanging woman, it was just the two of them in the glass house of Tooke. He went to the radio in the corner and turned it off. The violins faded, leaving only the creaking of the rope.

There was nothing more to be done but to alert the authorities and say that another death had occurred at Turnglass House. He would let them take her down – it seemed more respectful, although he couldn't say why. He went to the telephone in the hallway, all the while concentrating on the words to use: *I've gone to my friend's house. There's a woman here. She's hanged herself.*

But he stopped. Had she? He couldn't know that for certain. Around the Tookes, the more you knew, the less certain you became.

There was no sign that anyone else had been there, though. And when you added in the point that Alex's disappearance sure looked to have been on her hands and conscience, you did come to a conclusion. Sin, guilt, they had chewed her up over the decades to such a pitch that she had seen her dead son come to visit her. Who wouldn't have wanted that to stop?

He lifted the handset of the hallway phone.

'Operator,' announced a tinny voice.

'Police emergency.'

'Hold the line.'

He listened to a series of clicks. How long would it take for the . . .

He froze. There was the sound of footsteps outside, and then a key in the lock. And then Coraline was stepping inside. She was about to speak when he stopped her.

'Coraline,' he began urgently. But he softened. 'I have something to tell you.'

She looked at him with an inscrutable expression, something withheld. There was always so much she was holding back. 'How did you get in?' she asked.

He brushed the question away. 'The back door was open. But listen . . .'

'I closed that.'

'I came in and I found something here.' She waited. 'I found your mother.'

'Mama? She's here?' Coraline began to move into the house. 'Father only brought her over a few days ago. He said he'd keep her somewhere safe.'

He barred her path. 'Coraline, I'm sorry.'

'Sorry about what?'

'I found her dead.'

Coraline took a step back, staring into his face, attempting to find something there. 'What are you talking about?' she demanded.

Guilt, he thought to himself. *I'm talking about guilt.*

He put his hands on her shoulders, as if to steady her. It was the second time he had told her of the death of someone close to her. It was the second time he had been the one to find the body.

'She's hanged herself.'

There was silence for a while. Then a single word that was more cold breath than sound. 'Where?'

'Your bedroom.'

'Is she still there?'

'Yes. I just got here a few minutes ago.' He put his hand on her arm, an attempt at sympathy that brought no more response than if she had been made of glass too.

She placed her purse on a mahogany table beside the door and then, without looking at him, as if she had forgotten his presence entirely, went up to the bedroom. He saw her stop outside the room, looking in. She waited for a while, facing where he knew the body to be turning on the rope,

207

then crossed the threshold out of his sight. He gave her a few moments alone with her mother before he joined her.

It was an ugly scene.

'We need to take her down,' she said flatly.

'Yes.'

He could see the folds in Florence's clothes, her hair in disarray. And as the rope spun, her face slowly turned towards him. It had been lovely once; now it was aged by time and bloated by death. He reached to the cotton of her dress, holding it to keep the body still.

'Well?' Coraline asked. The sound filled the room.

'She's warm,' he said by way of an answer.

'So that means . . .'

'It's a warm day. I don't know how this works, it could make a big difference. But yes.' He knew her meaning and he met her gaze. 'I don't think she's been dead for long.'

Coraline sat on the sofa in the corner of her room, with her elbows on her knees.

'So if we'd come back a few minutes ago, we could have kept her alive.'

'You mustn't think like that.'

'Mustn't I? Who the hell are you to tell me how to think?' It was a rare flash of open anger. 'I want her cut down,' Coraline said.

'I know. But I . . .' He was interrupted by the sound of the bell at the front door. Coraline's head snapped around to stare towards the lobby. 'Who's that?'

'I don't know.'

The bell rang again. Then there was a thudding on the wood and a gruff voice. 'Police. Open up, please.'

As soon as Ken opened the door, he recognized the man. It was Jakes, the detective who had come when Oliver's body had been found.

'Detective,' Ken said, surprised.

'What's happenin'?' Jakes said, straight to the point.

'A woman's killed herself.' He couldn't understand why Jakes was there before he had even alerted the cops, but he would ask that question later.

'Here?' There was only a flicker of surprise. A man who had seen it all, for sure.

Ken led him up. 'Mary and Joseph,' Jakes muttered to himself when he saw the rope and what it held. 'Who is she?'

'My mother,' Coraline replied.

'Your mother?' He looked back up at the body, still now, the warm breeze having fallen away.

'She was in a mental institution in England. My father just brought her back home.'

A light of recognition and understanding seemed to fall on the policeman. No, this wasn't his first suicide. 'You told her about your brother's passin', ma'am?'

'Yes.'

Jakes sighed sadly. 'Figures. Sorry to say, but I've seen that before. No mother should bury her child. Were you the one who called?'

'Called?' she replied.

'Someone called the switchboard a half hour ago. Said I was needed here urgent. Wouldn't say why.' So, someone had called the police before Ken had entered the house.

'Who was it?' Ken asked.

'No idea.' He looked at Coraline. 'Definite wasn't you?'

'I told you, no.'

He stared up at the body above them. 'You think it was her?'

'How would she know your name?' Ken answered.

'Hard to say, but not impossible. I was the detective on your friend's case, after all.' The rope creaked. 'Let's get her down.'

Ken supported her torso as Jakes untied the rope and lowered her to the ground. All the while, Coraline stayed on the sofa, her elbows on her knees. Ken wondered how much of the wall of frost that surrounded her was a real part of her, and how much was thrown on each morning for protection.

'I'll call it in,' Jakes said. As he left the room, he stopped. 'I'm sorry, ma'am. No family should go through this much.' Then he went downstairs and they heard him call back to the station for a police ambulance.

They all waited without speaking, sometimes looking out to sea.

When the ambulance came, the two officers within it entered respectfully into the room, examined the body and slotted together a stretcher.

'Someone has to tell your father,' Ken said.

'I'll call him. I've done it before.'

'Detective!' One of the two officers placing Florence on the stretcher, kneeling at her side, called to Jakes, who was noting something in his pad.

'Hold on, I'm busy.'

210

'You want to take a look at this.' Ken moved towards the body. 'Please stay away, sir.'

'What is it?' Jakes asked.

'Look at this.' The officer lifted the dead woman's wrists.

Jakes sat on his haunches and pulled back the cotton cuffs. He nodded to his brother officer, who placed the wrists back at the sides of the woman's body.

'Mr Kourian,' he said. 'You found the body of Oliver Tooke, didn't you?'

'You know I did.' He didn't like the cop asking questions they both knew the answer to.

'And you say he was dead when you got to the scene.'

'What of it?'

'Well, now you also say that Mrs Tooke was dead when you got here?'

'That's right.' He could hear a tornado coming towards him.

'Did someone let you in?'

'No, I came in through the back door. It was open.'

'Open, huh? Is that normal?' He looked to Coraline for an answer, but didn't wait for one. 'And Mrs Tooke hanged herself.'

'She . . .'

The tornado hit. 'Then if Mrs Tooke hanged herself, you want to tell us just how she came to have rope burns on her wrists?' He left the words hanging in the air before he lifted Florence's arms, peeled back the material and showed the deep red welts that ran around her flesh. There was blood where they had broken through the skin. His tone fell. 'You want to tell us where that rope is now?'

Ken had known that Florence might not have taken her own life, but he hadn't put that alongside his own presence in the house, his thief-like entry through the rear door and the anonymous call to Jakes. Nothing good was coming from that. 'Someone wants you to think I killed her,' he said.

'Then someone's doin' a damn fine job of it. Anyone know you were comin' here tonight?'

Ken wracked his brain, which was running at full tilt on the back of being accused of a double murder. Other than Coraline herself, he had told no one. 'No. But they could have followed me.'

Jakes stood up and advanced half a pace. 'Followed you? And run in the house, killed her and run right out again without you seein'? That's fast work.'

He was right, of course. But Ken was thinking on his feet. 'Okay, maybe it wasn't me they were after. Maybe they were trying to put Coraline in the frame.' They all looked at her.

'You know anyone who would do that?' Jakes enquired.

She shook her head.

'Look, detective,' Ken insisted. 'You don't know that those marks happened while she was dying. They could already have been there. Or who knows, maybe someone did murder her, but it wasn't me!'

Jakes stared into Ken's eyes. 'I get a call sayin' I need to get here pronto. And when I do, I find you lookin' pretty cut up that I'm here, and the lady dead. How d'you think that looks to me?'

'Like a set-up!'

Jakes continued as if he hadn't heard. 'And somethin' else that's been on my mind.'

'What?'

'Table over there. Turned over and everythin's smashed.'

Ken looked at the table of perfume bottles he had knocked over when he entered and saw Florence hanging in the air. 'What of it?'

'It's what we call "sign of struggle". Makes me very suspicious.' His index finger pointed to Ken's chest. 'You're comin' in.'

'I'm not.' Ken was angry, and worried too. He couldn't deny how it looked.

'Then I'm arrestin' you on suspicion.'

'Suspicion of what?'

'You know what.'

The other officers were standing behind Jakes, watchful gazes fixed on Ken. One – he could have been twenty, maybe twenty-five – stepped forward, looking like he wanted to make an impression. He took hold of Ken's arm. Ken shook it off. The cop stepped right in, toe-to-toe, and Ken's blood was hot. 'You'd better step back, officer,' he growled.

'Or what?' He pushed Ken backwards, daring him to fight back.

'I said—'

'Or what?' and he moved to do it again.

But now Ken's blood was on the boil. So when the cop's chest shoved forward, Ken's right fist curved straight up from his hip, punching under the policeman's chin, knocking him to his knees. He sprang up and grabbed Ken around the neck, but before it could get any worse, Jakes had jumped in and wrenched them apart.

'Easy,' the detective warned them both. 'Neither of you do somethin' I gotta make a written report about.'

Ken thought for a second of running for the open door behind him. Two homicides would carry a court-ordered death sentence, no doubt about that. He could dash across the road into the forest and hide. But then what? Live out his life in the undergrowth? No, for now he had to play the game.

'All right. Get on with it,' he muttered. They snapped on a pair of handcuffs and pulled him away. He saw Coraline's face as he was led out. It was like she was seeing him for the first time.

When a paddywagon arrived, he was pushed in to sit on a metal bench screwed to the side. A steel wall separated the driver from the back where he was locked in. 'Watch him close,' Jakes ordered the policeman at the wheel.

'Won't get far with the bracelets on,' the officer replied. The young cop who had wanted the fight jumped in the front.

'Just watch him.' And Jakes went to his own car to lead the way.

With a whine of the engines, they all pulled out onto the road. A panel slid open and the face of the young cop appeared. 'Say, you ever been for a rough ride before?' he asked with a snigger. He didn't wait for a response. 'Hope you like it.' The panel slid back into place and, within a second, Ken felt the van swing right across the road, slamming him shoulder-first against the opposite side of the vehicle. There was nothing to grab hold of to steady himself. Immediately, the action was reversed and the van veered back to its first lane. The floor seemed to fall away from him and he tumbled backwards, the back of his head cracking against the steel bench. He nearly blacked out with the pain. In a second, the van swung again and his cheekbone cracked into a metal cuff, though he barely noticed it as they bounced over a hole in the road, lifting him into the air and then hard down onto the floor again. Without warning, the driver slammed on the brakes, shooting Ken into the dividing wall. He felt something in his nose crumple, and as he slumped down something warm was running down his chin. He heard laughter from the front as the van moved off again.

Laugh it up, boys, he thought to himself. *One day, I'm going to track you down and take you for a ride myself.*

Eventually, the gasoline fumes and angry traffic sounds told him they were in the city. Every one could have been a warning bell and he took them seriously. He was innocent, but he wouldn't be the first blameless man dropped into a prison grave. He sat hunched against the side of the van, his face bust up.

It seemed crazy. Just weeks ago, he had been living his dream: acting in the talkies; boating with good friends. Now his face would still light screens across the nation, but it would be a newsreel as he was strapped to a chair, waiting for the lethal vapour to overwhelm him.

To hell with it. He refused to crawl into self-pity. Someone would be going down for these crimes, but he was damned if it was going to be him.

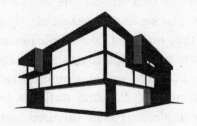

Chapter 18

At the station house, Jakes stopped to look at Ken's bruised cheeks and glanced at the two cops who had brought him in. He didn't look pleased. Ken had his fingertips inked and rolled on paper to record their prints. Then he was led through the back, into a room that contained nothing but a table and four chairs, all bolted to the ground. Jakes stood over him with his arms folded.

'I want a lawyer,' Ken said.

'Man tells me he wants a lawyer, I think he's done somethin' he needs a lawyer for.'

'Nice try, but I want to see one.'

Jakes leaned his knuckles on the table. 'If you're innocent, you'll want to clear everythin' up sooner rather than later.'

'*I want to see a lawyer.*' He said it slowly enough for the dumbest cop to understand, and Jakes didn't seem dumb at all.

The detective cussed under his breath and left. For an hour, Ken sat or paced around. He had nothing to do but think. Had someone deliberately set him up? The phone call to Jakes sure pointed in that direction. It was possible that a passer-by or neighbour had heard screaming or the like from the house and alerted the police, but they would have left their name.

Eventually, Jakes led a dark man into the room, a fat fellow carrying food stains on his shirt and a canvas bag full of bundled papers. 'Your lawyer,' Jakes said. 'Now, you got two minutes with him before I'm back and we talk.'

As soon as he had closed the door, the man, who introduced himself as Vincenzo Castellina, spoke in a machine-gun fire of words. 'Don't tell me if you did it or not. I don't care. I'm your lawyer. I'll do whatever I can to get you out.'

'I didn't do it,' Ken told him.

'You just broke the first rule. From now on, you do as I say. Got that?'

'Okay.'

'The cops do that?' He pointed to Ken's bust face.

'Sort of. Two cops and a ten-ton paddywagon.'

'Figures. Rough ride. Nothing you can do about it,' Castellina continued, hardly drawing a breath. 'The police told me what they got. It's probably insufficient to press charges. But first we gotta go through an interview. Don't worry, with me here they won't get rough.'

'Do they often?'

'Get rough? Sure. Usually on the hop-heads and queens. The spooks, now they get it the worst. You, you're okay. Wholesome white boy. So—'

He clammed up as Jakes re-entered. 'Had enough time to talk? Good.' He sat down on the other side of the table. 'Why'd you do it, Ken? What'd she do?'

'Having taken legal advice, my client will exercise his right to silence under the Fifth Amendment,' Castellina said authoritatively. 'He has committed no crime.'

'That true, Ken?'

'Having taken legal advice, my client will exercise his right to silence under the Fifth Amendment.'

'Can talk for yourself, can't you?'

'Having taken legal advice, my client will exercise his right to silence under the Fifth Amendment.'

It was obvious this stonewall was the lawyer's favourite tactic and had probably gotten him through a hundred such interviews. And it came out again and again for the next hour. At one point, another officer entered and handed Jakes a note.

'We spoke to Governor Tooke,' Jakes said, after reading it carefully and showing none of the tiredness that was by then hanging off the faces opposite him. 'He says he barely knows you. You been spendin' a lot of time around his family, though.'

'Having taken legal advice, my client will exercise his right to silence under the Fifth Amendment.' Even Castellina's voice was showing signs of strain after uttering the same sixteen words over and over.

Jakes folded the note and placed it in his pocket. 'You and his son. Somethin' between you, was there? You and him? You two have a tiff? What about the mom? You try it on with her? Keep it in the family? She look easy to you?'

At that dreck, Ken broke.

'Look, detective,' he burst out, 'I had nothing to do with the death of Oliver or Florence Tooke.'

'Say nothing,' Castellina ordered him.

Ken ignored him. 'Someone, somewhere, is setting me up for this.'

Castellina threw up his hands and Jakes went for a kill. 'Sure. Why didn't you call emergency when you say you found her? You just sit around takin' a look.'

'I started to, but Coraline came home. Then you turned up.'

'Yeah, you weren't expectin' that, were you? Funny thing, you hardly knowin' this family and suddenly you find two of them dead. Just you there, nobody else,' Jakes said, his voice a low threat.

'Not funny at all.'

'And while we're just shootin' the breeze, you want to tell me what happened with Mr Tooke? The deceased one?'

Ken had been hoping for a chance to float an idea; this wasn't how he had imagined it, but it would do.

'Okay, I will,' he said. 'The fact is, I think that he had something arranged that night, a meeting. If the man had come to the house, Coraline and I would have heard him come in, so Oliver must have met him outside. And he must have trusted this man some of the way, or he wouldn't have taken him out to the writing tower.'

'Of course. All part of some plan to kill Mr Tooke, an' the victim played along.'

'No, I don't think that was the plan.'

'Fill me in, why don't you?'

'Because if that was the case, wouldn't the killer do it in a less dramatic way? Knock him out while they're on the water and push him over the side so it looks like an accident. So no, I don't think it was always going to end that way. Some kind of negotiation that went sour would be my guess.'

'Negotiation.' Jakes's tone was one step short of outright mockery.

'Something like that. Then the other man took the boat back and left. The launch was at the beach – I guess it could have drifted there if Oliver hadn't tied it up, but the tide would more likely have taken it some way down the coast.'

'Oh yeah?'

'Yeah.'

'You a sailor?'

'No.'

'Then how the hell can you say what the tides are gonna do?'

'I'm not an idiot. And while we're talking about transport, there's another thing.'

'Sure there is.'

'When I went to the house tonight, I took a cab. The cabbie can tell you that I got there minutes – just minutes – before you did. Not enough time to do anything you suspect me of. Find him.'

'Maybe we will, maybe we won't.'

Their chests were heaving, like they were fighting for real.

Castellina intervened. 'Detective, do you have any evidence linking Mr Kourian to either crime? Actual evidence, not empty conjecture?'

'Empty conjecture, huh?' Jakes paced to the side of the room and folded his arms. 'Right now? No.'

'In that case—'

'But we got enough to hold you while we take a look-see.'

'What does he mean?' Ken asked Castellina.

The lawyer looked put out. 'You're dropping him in the can?' He glanced sideways at the bruise on Ken's cheek.

'Finest hotel in Los Angeles. No charge. And you know what, Ken? When we do find that evidence, you'll be for the gas chamber.'

His words had the confidence of a prediction.

Jakes banged on the door and a custody sergeant took Ken away.

He was led out past the front office, where a bar fight had brought in an army of rowdy drunks, and down through the bowels of the station. The floors smelled of bleach as if they had to be disinfected five times a day. There was no natural light; it was all from a line of caged-in bulbs and even they looked like they had seen better days. From time to time, one of the circling gnats would throw in the towel and land on a bulb to fry.

The sergeant led him through a door, where Ken found himself in a room so bright it hurt his eyes. It took him a second to realize that there were at least a dozen desk lamps all shining straight at him. Hands he didn't register shoved him into a cell, where he dropped onto a wooden bench covered with a stained white sheet that stank of human waste.

He was in the middle cell of three that lay along one side of a larger room, he saw, and a dozen cops were staring at him, stock still like vultures. One, a heavy-set man with bushy side-whiskers, opened his mouth to speak.

'You been places you're not wanted.' The cop looked up and down the bars, as if seeing them for the first time. 'Gotta keep animals in a cage.' Ken's nose rankled at something. There was a bucket beside the bench with the stench of a sewer. 'We'll watch you. All night long.' At that, he ran his nightstick along the bars and left the holding room. His footsteps echoed along the corridor, fading away to nothing, and one by one the other officers went back to their paperwork or reading newspapers or picking their teeth.

The calm before the storm. Where the hell was he going from here?

'Hey, boy,' a voice whispered. The words belonged to an old man with a shock of silver hair and tan skin that suggested he had some Indian in him, who was sitting on an identical stained bench in the cell to his left. 'They really got it in fo' you!' he said, and his mouth cracked open to show a line of black stumps. He fell back against the bars of his cell, laughing hysterically. One of the cops watched and laughed along.

Nobody offered him food or drink and he didn't ask for

any. He lay on the bench, trying not to think what the rag that covered it had been used for. *You been places you're not wanted.* That's what the cop had said. Was he talking about Ken being at the Tooke house that evening, or did it mean that someone didn't like how he had been sniffing around since Oliver's death?

What would Coraline be doing now? Would he be charged? Would his lawyer be able to get him out on bail? There were a ton of questions and not one answer.

Time stretched out. The number of officers thinned to one old man who reeked of garlic when he sauntered around past the bars of the cell, parading his own freedom as the only entertainment he had. Not even a radio would work down where they were, and the old geezer didn't look the type to enjoy a good book. At ten, the lights were switched off. After a couple of hours, Ken's mind gave up on racing between England and doctors and trick-books and men in boats; and sleep grabbed hold of him.

He wasn't sure what it was that woke him. It could have been the breath in his face, it could have been the hands on his wrists and ankles. More likely, it was the arm across his throat, cutting off his air.

His whole body jerked as if he had been hit by lightning. But the weight of men on him held him down, pressing him into the wood of the bench. His eyes were open, but he could only see dark shapes moving over him. He twisted his neck and tried to yell out, to shout an oath or call for help, but something wet and tasting of gasoline was stuffed in his mouth so that his tongue was smothered. And then there was the crunch of impact on the side of his head. And again on his stomach, with knuckles compacted into a fist. He groaned, but it made no noise through the wet rag in his throat. He struggled as hard as he could for what he guessed was his life, managing to drag free one fist that connected with soft tissue above him. Someone yelped like a kicked dog, but Ken's arm was grabbed again and pinned to the bench.

And then something snaked around his neck and tightened. It was rough, scratching into the skin as it bit tighter and tighter. A rope.

'Been places you're not wanted.' The murmur was loud in the still air. He could feel the snake around his neck squeezing. Soon it would squeeze so tight that the blood wouldn't flow. This putrid underground was going to be his coffin. 'But soon it won't matter.'

He could feel the blood in his veins fighting against the rope, a pulse choked off. His brain was getting slower without the oxygen. The dark was getting darker. What could he do? He only had a few breaths left before he would lose consciousness. It was his last chance. Through force of will, he concentrated his mind. He had to change the game. He couldn't speak and couldn't force them off. But he could confuse them. And so, from violently struggling, he went completely limp and held his breath, collapsing into the bench and letting his head roll to the side. There was a pause, then a change came over the men holding him.

'What happened?' he heard a light voice say. 'He have a heart seizure or somethin'?'

The hands on him stayed where they were – the cops

weren't stupid – but they loosened their grip. And then there was cautious movement above him: a patch of pure black moving against slate grey. He heard breathing coming closer. He could smell sweat, and old food on the man's breath. Closer, until he was close enough to listen for Ken's breathing. And with all his strength, Ken jerked his body up and his forehead forward to crack straight into the man's face with the force of a sledgehammer. There was a roar of pain as the cop staggered back. 'Kill this ...!' he yelled. And then the room was flooded with burning light that caused them all to wince.

'That's enough,' Jakes barked from the doorway, his hand dropping from the switch.

'He just—' bawled the cop, holding his face like a broken egg.

'He just nothin',' Jakes ordered him. And the look the other cop gave him could have killed. 'I said, he just nothin'.'

The other men muttered, spat on the floor and retreated. Ken reached up and tore the rope from his neck. It had been twisted into a noose. He threw it at the feet of the officer he had head-butted – the heavy-set one with thick side-chops.

'Yeah, well,' the cop said. 'Don't matter. Now or 'nother time.' And he swaggered out of the cell, followed by the others. They went to their seats and sat, watching him, as if it was just another day at work.

'You're out,' Jakes told Ken. He jerked his head towards the corridor. 'But you'll be back. We ain't found that cab driver of yours, an' somethin' tells me we won't.' Ken heaved himself to his feet. The strangulation had left him giddy and it was an effort to walk. As he passed Jakes, the detective spoke again. 'Tell me the truth 'bout what you did, or maybe next time I won't be here.' Ken shook his head. There was no point appealing for any understanding.

As he reached the corridor, he heard one of the cops call out, 'You wanna lay charges?' The others laughed.

Cops were corrupt, lazy, often stupid. He knew that. But as he stepped outside, he couldn't get his head around the fact that a squad of them were prepared to kill him too. Any point reporting them? None. All Ken would get out of giving a statement to the higher-ups would be to make sure he rose up their hit list.

No, his best bet would be to finish what he had started. Someone had set the dogs on him. He had to find out who was holding their leash.

Ken might as well have been drained of blood by the time he got back to his lodging house. The cops had decided that the contents of his wallet should go to their retirement fund, so he had had to walk all the way, among the booze-hounds and real criminals who took the Los Angeles night as their playtime. All he wanted was to lie down and sleep. He might not even get undressed. In the hallway, his landlady, perfectly made up and rouged as if it was early evening, instead of the small hours of the morning, stopped him in his tracks. Music came from her apartment and a man's seated legs were just visible through the doorway.

'Mr Kourian. You look ready to drop to the floor,' she said.

'I've had a hard day, Madame Peche.' It was lucky the light was low enough to hide his bruises. They were turning into real peaches and he didn't want to have to explain them.

'You have been working long hours. Or have you perhaps found a little friend?' She had a twinkle in her eye.

Well, let her keep her little fantasy.

'Working too hard.'

'Oh, that is a pity.' She went back to her rooms and he climbed the stairs. Each one seemed steeper than the last. As he was about to fit his room key into the lock, he stopped. He thought he had heard a sound from within. Something shifting about on the creaking floorboards. He listened harder. Nothing now. He tried the handle. It turned, but the door was locked as it should be. Relaxing, he pushed the key in and was about to twist it, but stopped again. This time, the sound was unmistakable: wooden, a sliding sound. He threw the door open and scanned the room. It was neat as he had left it, but the window was open. He rushed over and looked out. At first, he saw nothing except the surrounding buildings and rooftops, lit by streetlamps and house lights. Then he looked straight down. Below his window, the house had a small extension that Madame Peche used to store broken furniture, boxes of winter clothes and the like. And crouching on it, pressing himself into a nook, was the figure of a man, lit by a streetlamp. He wore a light suit and a flat felt cap with a peak that hid his features. But then he chanced a glance upwards, exposing a face extraordinary in its ordinariness – as if he had been specially bred so that no one could describe him to a police artist.

At the sight of Ken, he scrambled to the edge of the building and dropped to the ground, before dashing towards the main road.

For a split second, Ken thought about jumping down from the window and running after him, but from this height he would as likely break an ankle or his neck and he wasn't in the mood to do the guy that kind of favour. He charged down the stairs instead.

'Mr Kourian, what . . .' his flustered landlady voiced as he burst past her. He raced out onto the street, looking in every direction.

There! On the other side of the street, walking quickly but not running, a man in a light grey gabardine suit. No cap, but he had likely thrown that aside. 'Hey!' Ken cried. He sprinted over. The man started sprinting, too, down a long alleyway between high buildings. Ken rushed in his wake, his heart beating faster than a regimental drummer boy.

The alley was full of trash, and a nest of rats squealed as he leaped over them. The man he was chasing had pace, for sure, but instead of running out the other end of the alley, the man ducked through the doorway of a derelict timber building that was more rot than wood.

Ken reached the entry and stopped. The guy could be armed – more people bought guns than bought candy in LA these days – and there was no one else in sight. But the fight had come to his home now, so he wasn't going to back off and hope it all went away.

He trod carefully. It was a big building – it had been some kind of warehouse or factory. Shards of glass splintered under his feet as he entered. All the windows were filthy or broken and the dimmest glow from the streetlamps was filtering in. Some hulking piece of machinery at the side of the room was covered by a sheet and there was an empty doorway at the other end that looked like it led to a stairwell.

Ken stopped and listened. There was something that could have been wind through a broken-down building or the breath of a panting man. He moved in, his tread making only a light tap as he went. There had to be at least one other way out of the building and he wanted to trap his rat. He went towards the doorway at the end, but as he was about to reach it, he stopped. A slight rustling had caught his attention, like the movement of textile. He looked over to the covered machinery. Slowly, he went back to it. It was seven or eight yards square and a couple of yards high. The dirty sheet thrown over it was torn here and there. Ken picked a stone from the floor, one of those that the local boys had used to smash some of the windows. It would do as a weapon.

Was his quarry hiding inside the machine? Ken took hold of the sheet and pulled. It wouldn't come down. As he looked up, something fell towards him, blocking out the ceiling. It fell swiping at him with a heavy metal tool, cracking into his temple, knocking him to the floor, where he sprawled. The pain seared, pinning him to the ground. So when it had abated enough that he could stand to lift his head, it was only to see the figure sprinting away.

He could have staggered to his feet, but he was in no shape to give chase. He lay back on the smashed glass and let the waves of pain wash back over him.

It crossed his mind to report all this to Jakes, but would the detective believe him? Not for a single second.

Back in his room, having drawn the blind and waited a few minutes to make sure no one was waiting to burst in, he reached under his bedframe. He had tied something to the middle slat with thread and now he pulled it out. It was a small, oval, china object, inlaid with delicate mother-of-pearl lines: the holder of miniature pictures painted by Florence that he had found in the house on Ray. He carefully opened the egg-like item to reveal the two images inside: the house in Essex, the house in California, head-to-tail.

The artist had talent. Ken turned it around, so that the two houses flipped. But as it turned, he heard something that he hadn't noticed before: a slight ticking sound, like thin wood tapped by a nail. He spun it again and it happened again. There was something behind one of the pictures.

With the edge of a spoon, he carefully lifted the California picture from its housing. Nothing there. He did the same to the other side. This time, when the picture of the Ray house came away, there was something. It was a tiny model of a horse, carved out of wood, half an inch long. The sort of thing a child might have as part of a nursery menagerie. Wrapped around the horse was a thin slip of paper. Ken unfurled it:

Oliver, my brother. Sleep well.
Alexander

Alexander. He had written this.

And what was unmistakable was that the handwriting was neat and sloping. It wasn't the kind of scrawl that a four-year-old drags across a page. An adult had written this note.

Ken took the little model horse between his forefinger and thumb and held it up to the electric light. The wood was reddish brown and had a faint smell of ripe apples. What was that about a foal in Oliver's book? He grabbed his copy from the trunk. Yes, a foal had been put out of its misery and Simeon shown the carcass.

'Lame fro' birth. Best thin' for 'im,' Cain informed him.

Ken stared at the miniature for a long time. In its shadow was the truth about why Oliver had died. And Ken was beginning to see it.

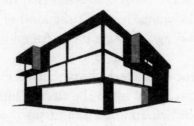

Chapter 19

The radio was playing in the background as Ken ate breakfast, squawking out band numbers alternated with a warning of severe weather on its way. The tropical storm building a few miles out to sea was expected to hit that night. No one knew how bad it was going to be, but every hour the weather service said that it was getting heavier and nastier. Householders should put up storm shutters on their windows. Children should be kept indoors and adults should leave home only if absolutely necessary. That wouldn't be popular.

He finished his toast and jelly, musing over the fact that he had resigned – well, kinda – from his job. He wouldn't miss it, but he regretted losing access to the newspaper's archive. He wanted to see again the stories he had been given about the family tragedy that had wrapped around the Tookes. No, he *needed* to see those stories.

So after clearing up, he headed over to the office, keeping a look-out for anyone he actually worked with who might question his presence in the building. He was lucky enough to get inside and down the stairs to the library without spotting anyone or being spotted.

'You brought me some cuttings about a kidnapping case back in 1915,' he told a malnourished man with a green dealer's visor.

'You here to complain?' He was at a desk in front of row upon row of bookshelves, each stuffed with large boxes. 'Only we're short-staffed. We can't send everything. You want cuts from the other papers, you need to spell that out and wait.'

Ken perked up at the information. 'You mean there might be more in other papers?'

'Sure. We got the back copies of the *Examiner*, the *Press* and the *Express*.'

'Can you get them for me?'

'What, all of them?'

'Is that possible? Just for 1915. No, make it '16, too.'

'Look, I got other work to do, you know.'

'Okay, I'll do it myself.'

The man in the green visor jerked his thumb towards the shelves. 'Knock yourself out.'

It took Ken a long while just to find the right volumes. The *Press* and *Examiner* had no more details than the *Times* had provided. But the *Express* had really gone to town. It had sent a reporter to talk to everyone and anyone connected to the story, and returned to it whenever it had an excuse. And there was a name, buried deep in one of its articles, that Ken recognized. It was from the 1916 batch, after the family had returned from Europe. There was a photograph of them pushing Oliver in a wheelchair towards an office that he also recognized.

> Some good news at last for the tragic Tooke family. After the shock of his brother's terrible kidnapping, little Oliver Tooke is seen being taken to the surgery of society doctor Arnie Kriger [the reporter had mis-spelled his name, but it was clear who they were writing about]. Kriger is an expert in childhood diseases. One of his staff told the *Express* that the boy's polio had improved remarkably during his time in Europe and he might soon be able to walk, albeit with some difficulty. We at the *Express* pray that he does!

Ken wondered which nurse or receptionist had received a few creased dollar bills in return for that information. He packed up and returned home to work out what that story meant. He left a message for Coraline to call him. They needed to talk.

The storm hit that night.

Sheets of rain shot along the streets, throwing trees against walls, smashing through window panes. Anyone caught on the road – those who had missed the radio messages and the warnings in the newspapers – cowered in shop doorways, looking for a way out. When they tried to shout to each other, they could barely make a sound.

Ken stood in his room. His landlady had run about the house, handing out wooden boards to place inside the windows in case they shattered – it was too late to nail them across the outside. When the power had cut out, Ken had stumbled out onto the landing and found a candle.

He was deciding how best to hold back the flood when a frantic knocking sounded on his door, someone trying the handle, against the bolt. 'Who is it?' he called. He wasn't expecting anyone, so he was on his guard after the last unannounced visitor.

'Coraline,' came the answer.

He slipped back the bolt. The weather had soaked through her clothes and he watched the water trickle down her skin. Her air of sophistication was gone, leaving a natural beauty.

'Come in.'

'No. You have to leave. Now.'

He was alert. He had been through enough to know that the threats around him weren't idle. 'Why?'

'The police. Jakes called me. They have a witness who saw you arrive at the house with my mother. They asked me if I could explain that.'

'It's a lie,' he growled. He pulled her inside and shut them both in. 'I should have seen something like that coming.'

235

'I know it's a lie. But they told me something else.'

'What?'

'They found a knife, a lock-knife at the house. Kicked under the furniture, they said. It had white fibres in it that look like they're from cutting a rope like the one used to . . . kill her.'

'Okay, well . . .' He was about to say that the knife wasn't his. Then something struck him. He went to the trunk of his possessions and hunted through it.

'What are you looking for?'

He sat back on the bed. Now the break-in of his room made sense.

'I had a knife like that. I use it for meals. It's been taken.' A shadow of scepticism slipped across Coraline's face. 'Save it. I know how it looks. Some cops tried to kill me last night.'

'What?' Even with all the rest that had happened, she sounded amazed.

'Maybe they just wanted to scare me for punching that cop yesterday. I don't know. Anyhow, they held me down in the station and put a noose around my neck. That wasn't a barrel of fun.' He rubbed his throat. 'It could be they're in someone's pocket.'

'Everyone's in someone's pocket.' She paused. 'Will your fingerprints be on the knife?'

'Covered with them.'

'We have to go. Now. I've got Oliver's car.'

He grabbed a raincoat and hurried out with her, doing his best not to make an impression on the other residents, who were standing around with storm lamps and

236

armfuls of boarding. Madame Peche, carrying a heap of bedding that had been soaked through, stopped him on the stairway.

'Mr Kourian. You can't possibly be going out in this,' she told him.

'I have no choice.'

She stared at Coraline with an arched eyebrow. 'I see. Well, the door will be locked when you return this evening. *If* you return this evening.'

'I understand.'

They forced their way out into the torrent. It was coming straight down now, a mass of freezing water pouring from black clouds that had swamped Los Angeles. The power was out everywhere and the only light came from the gas streetlamps and flashes of lightning.

'The electricity's gone,' Coraline shouted.

'Lines must be down. It shorts out the whole city grid when that happens,' he cried back. 'Where's the car?'

She pointed to the other side of the street. The Cadillac stood idle in front of a liquor store. She slipped in the river coursing along the road and he caught her just as she fell.

They closed themselves in the car as a tree branch flew across the road, followed by other debris: a newspaper, some packaging, a billboard that would never convince anyone else to buy Johnson & Johnson's tooth powder.

Coraline started the motor. It must have been warm from the journey she had just made, although the water pouring through it threatened to seize it up.

He reached into his pocket and pulled out the china picture holder. 'You remember this from the house in Essex?'

'Of course. My mother's pictures. God knows why Oliver wanted to leave it in that wreck. God knows why anyone would want to be there at all.'

Ken opened it and lifted out the picture of the house on bleak Ray. The little horse lay nestled behind it. He took it out into the light. 'I think it's something to do with this. I found it last night. At first, I thought it was a horse.'

'It's not?'

'Not quite, it's a foal.' He didn't show her the slip of paper that had been wrapped around the model. The slip that read:

Oliver, my brother. Sleep well.
Alexander

'And the difference is?'

'Oliver's book. There's a foal in it. The foal dies. I had forgotten all about it until I found this. It seems so insignificant when you read the story. So I'm only now realizing what it really means. Oliver was clever. There are a lot of subtle messages in his book. But some are so subtle, only the person they are meant for would understand.'

'Tell me about this one,' Coraline said.

'There's something else we need to know first, but we'll find out tomorrow. And right now, we have to keep out of sight.'

They pulled into the street. The methane streetlights meant they could find their way on the road, but the water, six inches deep on the asphalt, slowed them down. They passed shut-up and shivering diners and stores, but had only gone a few streets when Coraline began checking over her shoulder.

'What is it?' he asked. He already had an idea what it was.

'There's about three cars on the road tonight,' she replied. 'I think the one behind us was parked outside your boarding house.'

He twisted around to see a racing green Desoto Sedan. Someone was screwing with his life, that was for certain. The chances were that it was either a cop or the plain-faced man in the gabardine suit who had previously paid him a visit. 'Are you sure?'

'No.' But Ken kept close watch on the vehicle for two more streets until Coraline took a sharp, last-second turn, spraying a thick wave of dirty water across the sidewalk, and the car made no attempt to follow. Whether it had been thrown off or they were imagining a threat where none existed, he couldn't tell. 'So, we keep running away,' she said.

'Listen. Whoever they are, they're after me, not you. I can get out here. I'll find my own way. You'll be safer.'

She turned the wheel and pressed the pedal. 'I doubt it.'

They drove, buffeted by the wind. Fence posts lifted into the air and cracked down onto the ground. Parked cars shook on their wheels and uncovered windows exploded into fragments. 'We should find somewhere to put in,' he said. 'Take the next right. There are some cheap hotels that way.'

'Wonderful,' she replied.

They hung a right, carried on a few blocks and found a row of flop-houses with names that promised luxury they couldn't even pretend to offer: The King's Hotel, Shangri-La, Excelsior Rooms. All would normally have been lit up, but the electricity grid was out and they looked like cemeteries.

They pulled into one that offered parking, a narrow brick building with an unfinished fire escape. It wasn't even clear if the hotel was yet to open or already closed down, but they took a chance.

Behind the front desk, a man was asleep on a mattress, his wire spectacles still on his nose, all dimly lit by a kerosene lamp. Ken smacked the bell and the night clerk, who smelled strongly of cheap sourmash, roused himself with a groan.

'Buck fifty per night. Hot water extra. Sign here,' he mumbled. 'Got a car?'

'No.' The clerk might take it upon himself to go out and take a look at the number plate.

'Fine. Cash up front.'

Ken handed over the money. The man either didn't notice or didn't care that they had no luggage. He handed them a grimy lamp and they climbed the steep stairs to their room.

It was a ten-feet-square firetrap. The bed was spread with two sheets that between them just about covered it.

'What do you think, Ken?'

Her hair was running with water, delicate beads falling to the floor. And the lamp flame lit her eyes so that he saw the room reflected in them; and he strode across and to hell with it and he pulled her by the shoulders so her mouth turned up to his and he pressed their lips together hard. She was warm and yielding; until she pulled back and away from him, dabbing her mouth with her sleeve.

'I'm sorry,' he said.

'Don't be,' she replied quietly. 'Another time and it would have been—'

'I know. I know what it would have been.'

'I guess I'm just the unlucky type.'

'I guess we both are,' he said, staring out at the dark.

Just as he was drifting off to sleep, Ken heard a new voice coming up from reception.

'Hello, Mick.'

'Hello yourself.' It was the night clerk's voice.

'We had a call come through. Looking for a couple. Twenties. Sound like swells. Could be driving. Anyone arrived in the last few hours?' Ken sat up, alert.

'Last few hours? I been asleep the last few hours.'

'That so?'

'Sure is.'

There was a pause. 'Yeah, well, holler if they turn up.'

'There a reward?'

'Reward? Sure there's a reward. The reward is we don't shut you down.'

The voices fell quiet. Then the stairs creaked. Someone was coming up. Ken jumped to his feet. There were bars across the window, so he would have to make a stand. The footsteps halted outside the room. Ken held his breath, ready for the cop to burst in. But it was the clerk's voice.

'Get the fuck outta here. I ain't seen you.' And the stairs creaked again as he returned to his post.

Ken pulled his jacket on again. They handed back the key, ran to the car and drove it out through the dirty river that used to be Los Angeles. They found a blacked-out, empty lot to park in for a few hours and wait, shivering, on the back seat. The clerk kept their money.

Chapter 20

The wind rolled all through the night, and morning meant no let-up. The solid clouds of the tropical storm – now threatening to turn into a hurricane, according to an excited newscaster on the car radio – meant the whole city was enveloped by a dark grey and lashed by streaming rain. Mid-morning was in twilight and the few cars about were trundling along with headlamps lit so they looked like hellish insects. The road ran with deep, muddy water. Ken parked the car in a spot where he could see their target.

'How long do we wait?' Coraline asked.

'Until he gets here.'

She lit a Nat Sherman. The gusts whipped away the

smoke as soon as it came close to the gap at the top of the car window.

They edged closer to each other, without thinking, to stay warm. It was impossible to see the sun; they could only tell by their wristwatches that it must be above them.

'There he is.' Ken pointed through the windshield, blurred as it was by the rain washing down. She nodded. The tiredness of the night was showing on her face.

Ken got out of the car and waited for the man on the other side of the road to open up his office. Then Ken charged across, into the doorway, barging him inside into a wide corridor and slamming the door after him.

'What are—'

Ken stopped the words with his fist. The doctor squealed in pain and fell back against the wall, holding his hand across his twisted mouth.

'No sound,' Ken warned. Kruger raised a palm in submission. 'I want to know about the Tooke family.'

'What . . . what can I tell you?'

'The mother. What was her mental condition after her son was taken?'

The doctor stammered, unable at first to form words. 'I'm not an expert in diseases of the mind.'

'Hazard a wild fucking guess.' He lifted his fist again.

'All right!' Kruger pleaded. 'She was distraught. Of course. Her son had gone.'

'She was eaten up by guilt, Doctor. And you know why. You know what she did.'

'I don't. *I don't*,' he protested.

Ken seized Kruger's shirt, twisted it in his fist and pinned the man to the wall. 'And the boys. What were they like?'

Kruger seemed relieved to move on to a new subject. 'They ... Alexander was healthy. Oliver exhibited severe poliomyelitis.'

'What was his prognosis?'

'What does it matter?' the man cried.

'*Answer the question.*'

Kruger threw up his hands in a second submission and gave an impressive performance of a man doing his best to recall facts from twenty-five years earlier. 'Probably a life-long cripple.'

'And what treatment did you recommend?' The man blinked nervously. But this was the crux of it all. This was where it had all gone wrong: for Oliver, for Alexander, for Coraline, for Ken. And he would rather stop Kruger from ever breathing again than let him swallow the truth. 'Tell me now or I'll break your neck in ten different ways.'

A few minutes later, Ken emerged from the building. He went to a telephone booth at the end of the street, where he made a call. Jakes answered and Ken told him a story.

'Oliver's book,' Ken said as he got back into the Cadillac. 'It's all in there if you look.'

'What is?'

'Everything.'

'Where are we going?'

'Back to your house.'

He gunned the engine and pulled out into the river-road.

A wave erupted against the side of the car as the wheels churned the water. The city was drowning, all under the pale amber light from the gas streetlamps.

'There's a car behind us,' she said quietly, her voice almost becoming lost in the rain.

'The same one?'

'Yes.'

He glanced at the wing mirror. He could make out a racing green Desoto. This time, there was enough light to see a man at the wheel. He was wearing a muffler, but Ken knew who it was. 'I thought he was gone,' he muttered. 'Well, we'll see how he drives.'

He stamped down the accelerator and the car jumped forward, skidding as it went.

'He's coming with us,' Coraline said, watching the other car over her shoulder. Ken spun the wheel, hanging around a corner, lifting the Cadillac's offside wheels a few inches from the ground and crashing them down again with a shockwave through the car. The Caddy had a more powerful engine than the Desoto and it quickly put distance between the two. But the conditions meant it couldn't tear away, and the Desoto began to gain. 'What does he want?' she asked.

'Us.'

The green car suddenly roared forward, finding a reserve of acceleration, and its front fender hacked at the Cadillac's rear, screwing the front car on a plane of water before Ken was able to right it again.

'What was that?' Coraline asked.

'He's trying to knock us off the road.'

The car behind gained again and thudded into them. Only this time, the two fenders locked into each other, twisting the cars into one hefty machine. Ken pressed and released the accelerator, but the Caddy was trawling a heavy burden. He turned left and right, attempting to shake loose, but it was no good. And now they were coming to a crossroads.

When Ken had been taught to ride, he had learned that when you take a corner, you lean into it and kick your heels into the horse's flank so the beast pushes harder. If you don't, you can be thrown off. It was the same with automobiles. Corners demanded acceleration, and as he reached the junction he put the pedal to the metal. The engine screamed, but the car behind was still holding them back. He hit the gas again, hard enough to put the pedal through the floor. Then, at the last second, he spun the wheel to the right, turning the car on a dime.

There was a bang and a tearing of steel, and the Caddy shot forward. The needle jumped up past fifty, and Ken whirled his head to see the other car spinning away, thrown off by the turning torque and the Cadillac's fury. It was skidding sideways across the wet asphalt, over the broad intersection and straight for the oncoming traffic. Those other vehicles shrieked to halts pointing in crazy directions, but still the Desoto skidded. And then its two left wheels simultaneously hit the opposite kerb, and the car burst upwards, a yard into the air, crashing into a streetlight and breaking it in two like a sapling, before dropping back onto the sidewalk to rest on its side.

Ken lifted his foot from the accelerator and rammed it

down onto the brake. The tyres screeched and smeared the road, stopping about twenty yards down the street. He jumped out, opened the trunk and grabbed a heavy wrench from the repair kit. He ran to the wrecked Desoto with it raised. Twenty, fifteen, ten yards. It took him seconds to sprint it. And as he came close, he saw the driver through the void where the windshield had been. There was blood on his face and for a moment Ken had no idea if he was alive or dead. The broken streetlamp was spewing gas, making the air stink of rotting food.

The man's torso was slumped across the two seats. 'Who are you?!' Ken shouted, ripping away the muffler. The bloody mouth was groggy, attempting to form words, then closing dumbly. 'Tell me!' He lifted his wrench, threatening more pain if the question wasn't answered.

The man's eyes narrowed a little. He reached forwards, towards Ken, shoving at the door. It was already half-open, the bottom of it torn by the crash so that metal ran in twisted spurs. It wouldn't open properly and one of the ribbons of steel scraped against another with a whine. The driver tried again with all his weight, and as the two strips of metal rubbed against each other little sparks flew up, sheltered from the weather by the automobile.

Ken dropped the wrench and stepped back. He could see that the danger wasn't the driver, but what was about to happen. Another burst of sparks and it did. The gas in the air ignited, and Ken hit the ground as the car was engulfed in a fireball five yards across. If the sun had dropped through the sky, it couldn't have burned brighter.

The rush of boiling air was like another gale, and when he lifted his head, he saw a jet of flame from the streetlamp rising ten feet into the dark storm.

He lay his head back down on the road. The man in the car was no threat now. He felt warm blood. A deep gash had opened on his cheek. It was as if, for a few moments, the whole world had collapsed in on itself. All he could do was take rattling breaths.

'Sir, are you okay?'

It was a woman, holding a hat on her head. 'Were you hit by the . . . the . . .' She searched for a word to describe what she had just seen.

'No,' he said quietly, feeling his lungs wheeze. 'I wasn't.'

He wiped his sleeve across his face, smearing ash over it. He dragged himself back to the car. Coraline emerged, shaken up. 'Was he the one who killed Oliver and Mama?'

'Probably.'

'Was he trying to kill us?'

'It doesn't really matter now.'

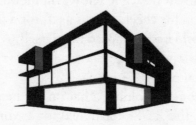

Chapter 21

The car glided through the iron gates of Turnglass House. The storm at sea could be seen right through the building.

The maid, Carmen, opened the door to them, then folded in on herself, instantly self-conscious, their last talk with her having revealed deeply hidden secrets.

'Where's my father?'

'The library, miss. But he's being interviewed for radio. And ...'

They ignored the warning and went upstairs. Governor Tooke was sitting in a red velvet wing-backed chair, with a microphone and recording equipment set in front of him. A young presenter had his own microphone.

'... KQW speaking to Governor Oliver Tooke, the frontrunner for the Republican presidential nomination. Governor, the storm is raging around us, but America's got a great future ahead of it. Wouldn't you say, sir?'

'Well, Mr Willett, I would say that. And that's because—'

'Father, we need to speak to you.' Coraline stared straight into his eyes without wavering or blinking.

'My dear, I'm speaking to—'

'It's about Oliver. And Alex.'

Tooke looked at her like she was a scorpion.

The radio man spoke. 'Sir, may we—'

'I think my daughter and I need to talk.'

The presenter looked unhappy with the situation, but took his cue and left the room.

Coraline went to the window, took a packet of cigarettes from her purse, lit the last one and stared outside. The Governor looked to Ken.

It was a sad and beat-up road they had travelled. Ken had begun it with a friend, but that friend had had his life stolen from him. And it had all begun with a boy's simple, common misfortune.

He sat in the radio presenter's seat.

'We have a difficult conversation to conduct, Mr Kourian. Is that not so?'

'It is.'

'Well, it's been some time coming, but come it must. Would you like a drink?'

'A drink? No, no, thank you, Governor.'

'It's very early, I know. But I think I might have one.'

He went to a large globe and lifted the top half to reveal glinting bottles. He took a couple out, setting them on the side table, but didn't open any. He was unsure. It must have been unnerving for him to be like that. And he returned to his seat without a glass.

Where to begin?

Ken chose to begin with the story.

'I read the last book Oliver wrote. It's a strange thing. Truly unique.'

'My son was a disapp—'

Ken cut him off. 'Your son was clever, that's what he was. His book took some unravelling.'

'Enlighten me,' Governor Oliver Tooke said, the displeasure returning. He glanced at his daughter. She met his gaze.

'I will. At its heart, it's a story about identity. About being two people at once. Not knowing who you are. And it's about a lame foal put to death in a stable.' Those details should have told him everything. But the truth was so extraordinary, who could have dreamed it? Ken paused and looked out the window. The Essex rain seemed to be running down the glass. Then he could stand waiting no more and asked, 'Why did you do it?'

'Why did I do *what*?' Tooke's jaw was set hard. The smoke rose from Coraline's cigarette and drifted among the books.

The harsh words, the condemnation, seemed to form not in that room, but outside, in the beating rain.

'Mr Tooke, I've been through a lot. I don't care for any more of this today. You had a man end the life of your polio-crippled elder child. And you raised your other son in his place, convincing the world for twenty-five years that he was his elder brother. Why?'

Tooke went back to the table that held the clutch of bottles. He selected a bottle of whiskey and splashed half the straw-coloured contents into two crystal tumblers. He offered one to Ken, who refused it.

'Ah well,' the older man said, returning one of the glasses to the side. 'Time's up.' He dropped into the wing-backed chair and drank a long draught. Enough to get most men drunk in the blink of an eye. 'Why, why, why.' He pointed a scrawny middle finger at Ken. 'Well, you know something? Times are changing, that's why. Once a man would be elected president by his peers – other sharp men who knew what was best for this country. Men who could read and write and think. Men who understood commerce and the law, and what rights a man should have. But now that's changed.' He believed what he was saying, that was clear. He was a man who believed with all his being. 'Now that voting has been extended to every man and woman who can put a cross on a ballot paper, it's whoever looks best on the newsreels and speaks the prettiest on the radio. He's not chosen on brains or ability, sir, he's cast like one of those flickers that you are so desperate to appear in. And that's a dangerous state for a country.'

'Is it?'

'Oh, oh yes, it is.' Tooke nearly laughed. On a run now. 'But I stand for something. I stand for the betterment of this country for the collective good of its people.' His hands knitted together to illustrate society united. 'And a nation is no more than its people; so we have

253

GARETH RUBIN

to make the *people themselves* stronger. Finer of mind and body.' Ken pictured Kruger entering the American Eugenics Society headquarters. That building was full of men who thought like Governor Tooke and had been encouraged by events in distant Germany to call openly now for what they believed. 'And I will not be a hypocrite. No, I will not. So I had to practise what I preach.' He took another swig.

'And so?'

'And so.' He lost himself in his thoughts for a moment. 'And so, I had my dear boy taken away, and I let my younger son take his place and his name.' It was the bitterest of vindications. It hung in the air for a while. Ken could hear it echoing. 'Like Abraham, I sacrificed my son. And yes, soon enough Alexander began to believe he was Oliver. He was four years old – you come to believe anything at that age darn quickly. He forgot very soon that we had ever called him anything else.' He swilled his drink around. 'Maybe at the back of his mind, there was always half a memory, I don't know.'

The storm battered at the walls, providing the only sound in the room. Until Coraline spoke. Ken could see the hate in her had turned cold. 'You were always so sure of yourself, Father. Morally. As if it oozed out of your pores.' She went to the drinks table and took the unclaimed glass of whiskey. She drank half without looking at either of them.

'Was it Kruger who took him away?' Ken asked.

'It was the kindest thing for him.'

'And how the hell do you figure that?' It seemed

impossible to Ken that they were sitting here discussing the death of a boy and that Tooke was talking like it had been no more than an unpleasant duty.

'Life as a cripple is no life.' He rolled the glass in his fingers. 'Do you want to try it, having others push you everywhere? Dress you? Take you to the bathroom? Watch your brother run on the athletics field you can't set foot on?'

He seemed, still, to believe every word he uttered.

'What about Mama?'

Tooke glanced at Coraline. 'She didn't want it, of course. Took some hard, hard persuading.'

'It sent her mad.'

'I did my best for her. Put her somewhere they would look after her well. Visited her when I could.' And for the first time, Ken heard the faintest tone of shame. The Governor lifted his glass to his lips, then placed it on the table. But it didn't sit properly and tipped over. He didn't try to right it.

'Christ,' Coraline said under her breath.

'Why the deception?' Ken said.

'What do you mean?'

He felt sick asking it, as if the mechanics of the Governor's actions were what mattered and not the outcome. 'When Kruger took him away, why did you pretend it was your younger boy who had been kidnapped? Why not just say it was the older one with polio who was gone?'

The wind was picking up. Rain was spattering the window, shaking it, threatening to rush right through.

'You tell me, Mr Kourian.'

He had been weighing that question for hours. And there was only one answer that fitted. 'I think it was because your views on eugenics were well-known. If your crippled son had disappeared in strange circumstances, suspicion would have fallen on you. Even if it couldn't be proved, that would have been the end of your political career. But this way ... this way, you actually gained sympathy.' The Governor made no reply. Ken hated to know that he was right. And that was why his friend, Oliver, had spoken of the guilt he harboured: because his life was a part of his brother's death. 'But everything changed when you saw Oliver's book. You read it and realized that he had found your wife and worked it all out. Didn't you?'

Tooke paused before speaking. 'Actually, you're not quite right there,' he said.

'I'm not?'

'Not quite. For all your cleverness, you're missing a nuance or two.'

'What nuance is that?'

The Governor huffed in scorn. 'My son. My last chance for a man to continue our line and he was no better than the pansies he associated with.' He looked to his side, as if searching for an explanation for how his own child had turned out to be such an embarrassment. 'And then, when he knew what he knew and he summoned up all the courage he had to face me, what did he do? He overshot. Played his hand too high.'

'What the hell are you talking about?'

Tooke looked Ken up and down like he was appraising an animal. 'What I am talking about, Mr Kourian, is that my milksop son was threatening me.'

'How?'

The Governor's pale hand reached for his desk drawer. The wood came out of its housing with a whine. Tooke held a copy of *The Turnglass* up to Ken, before tossing it aside like it was a disease. 'He said this was a taster of what was to come. When I ran for the White House, he was going to go to the police with the full story.' His forefinger jabbed back and forth as anger lifted his voice. 'He thought he would see me in handcuffs. Now! Just as I was about to save this nation from a devastating war against a friendly and admirable country. I could not let that happen.'

The rain washed down the pane. 'So you sent a man to frighten him into keeping quiet, but things got out of hand, maybe he fought back, and he ended up dead.' The Governor reached for the overturned glass, but his fingertips set it rolling over the edge of the table and it fell to the floor, breaking into a hundred pieces. 'Who was it you sent?' Ken asked.

'Does it matter?' The anger had ebbed away.

'Probably not. I think we met him tonight.'

'And?'

'You won't be seeing him again.'

'I see.' Tooke looked at the shattered whiskey glass. 'His family always worked for us. His grandmother was even in Oliver's book. The housekeeper. They always were loyal and I kept them that way.' A thought seemed

257

to come to him. 'Not that it really matters, but what have you done with Kruger?' A sudden burst of wind shook the window; there was a spider's web of cracks in one corner and the rain was seeping through.

'I called a policeman I know,' Ken informed him.

'Are they coming here?'

'Yes.'

The Governor sighed in tiredness, as if he had been awake for months. A clock in the corner passed into a new minute.

Coraline spoke. 'Grandfather would have drowned you if he'd known what you were going to do.'

'Oh yes, miss?' Tooke said bitterly. 'Well, here's something else you just won't credit. You know who is really behind what I did?'

'Tell me.'

'That would be your grandfather himself.'

Ken was struck. 'Simeon?' he said.

'You see, I know what Oliver wrote about our little family intrigue in the last century,' Tooke continued. 'But ask yourself this: where did he hear the story from? All from my dad, of course. And you think that man was telling God's own truth about what really happened? Oh no. I have my doubts about that. You read the story. Do you believe it? The woman running around London like the Lone Ranger, and the old man leaving all his worldly goods to a boy he had barely met? That doesn't strike you as bent out of shape? Oh no. No, miss. My father needed money for his cholera research and a way of getting it fell into his lap. Just a few days of treatment with who-knows-what and the inheritance was his for the taking. And then who is anyone to question his telling of history?'

Ken's mind tumbled. The book, with all its subterfuge, had been a trove of truth for him. But was it really? Maybe there was another layer of lies to dig through.

Tooke was calm as he continued. 'So you see, Mr Kourian, what my father did in that house before me showed me what I had to do there after his example. Because good men do what is right no matter what others would say about it. Like my father, and like Abraham.'

For a while, Ken watched him. There was a light behind the man's eyes that was beginning to flicker and dim. Then Ken spoke. 'Abraham didn't go through with it.'

'Excuse me?'

He met the Governor's gaze. 'He didn't go through with it. The angel of the Lord came down and stopped him. Isaac lived. It was only a test. Of faith.'

There was the muffled sound of an automobile engine. It was pulling up outside.

Tooke's fingers curled into his palms. 'Well, sir, that's fine for the Good Book. But here on earth,' he leaned in to make his point, 'a man's hand is bloodier.'

Ken didn't care about this man's weak, cheap pride. It meant nothing. 'You know, I think I only just understood what the story's about, the way Oliver wrote it,' he said. There was movement somewhere in the house now. The sound echoed off the breaking windows; tread on marble coming closer. 'It's not just about you, or your son, or your father, even. It's really about the past having a will of its own: a will to vindication. To retribution, I guess. The past always wants that.' The leaves of Oliver's book, lying on the cold floor, stirred slightly in the breeze. 'So you can bury it in bricks, or stone, or down in the mud; but when you do that, you only give it time, Governor.'

He watched the web of cracks spread through the glass. *Let it all come down now*, he thought.

THE END